Deadly

Deadly
DECEPTION

BETSY HAYNES

DELACORTE PRESS

Published by
Delacorte Press
Bantam Doubleday Dell Publishing Group, Inc.
1540 Broadway
New York, New York 10036

Book design by Claire Naylon Vaccaro

Library of Congress Cataloging in Publication Data

Haynes, Betsy.
Deadly deception / by Betsy Haynes.
p.   cm.
Summary: When her boyfriend is arrested and charged with murdering the school
guidance counselor, seventeen-year-old Ashlyn tries to find the real killer.
ISBN 0-385-32067-1
[1. Mystery and detective stories.   2. Murder—Fiction.]   I. Title.
PZ7.H314913De   1994

[Fic]—dc20   93-39011
                                                                                CIP
                                                                                 AC

Manufactured in the United States of America

June 1994

1   3   5   7   9   10   8   6   4   2

For Louise Eovaldi

Deadly DECEPTION

The ringing telephone blasted through the darkness like a siren. Instantly awake, I rolled over and glanced at the clock as I grabbed the receiver: 1:33. Who could be calling at this time of night?

"Hello?"

"Ashlyn, it's me." Keeley sounded upset.

I frowned at the clock again. Had I read it right? I had. "What's wrong?" I whispered.

"It's Drew. He's here and he needs you."

I sucked in a deep breath and sat up in bed, a knot forming in my stomach. "Drew? At your house?" I paused, knowing the answer to my next question before I asked it. "Why is he there in the middle of the night?"

"I thought you'd guess," Keeley said softly.

I leaned back against the rattan headboard and

closed my eyes, dreading to say the words out loud. "Andy's back."

"Right. At least I think so. Drew really isn't talking. That's what makes it so bad. He just sits there and stares at nothing. He won't say anything, and he won't leave. Oh, Ashlyn, you've got to come. He really needs you."

I heard the desperation in my best friend's voice. "My parents were already asleep when I looked out my bedroom window and saw his pickup out front," Keeley went on. "At least he's trying to get help. You have to give him credit for that much."

Even though Andy's back, I added silently. Part of me wanted to scream, "Tell him he can't do this to himself!" And part of me wanted to run to him and tell him everything was going to be okay. And that I'd help him and stick by him no matter how rough things got.

"Anyway, I went out and tried to talk to him," said Keeley. "I thought maybe you two had a fight or had broken up or something, so I asked him what was wrong, but he wouldn't say a word. So then I asked him if he'd like to spend the night in the dock house, and that's where he is. I think you'd better get over here. I don't know what he'll do. Or what he's already done."

I started to speak and then hesitated. I had heard something. "Uh-oh, Mom's on the prowl," I said as a sliver of light appeared under my door. "I have to go."

"But are you coming?"

"I'll try."

A split second after I replaced the receiver in its cradle the door opened, and my mother stood silhouetted against the light.

"Who in the world was that?" she asked, sounding alarmed. "Don't your friends know better than to call in the middle of the night?"

I winced at her words and squinted toward the dark figure outlined in the intense brightness. I knew she thought it was Drew. I couldn't understand why she didn't like him. Or at least give him a chance. She always acted as if he wasn't good enough. Drew Jansen, of all people. His great-grandfather had founded the town. Sighing, I murmured, "It was just a wrong number."

"At this hour?"

"He sounded drunk. Speaking of the hour, what's keeping you up so late?" I asked, trying to change the subject.

"I was finishing up work on the talk I'm going to give at the governor's task force this weekend. I had just turned off my light when I heard the ring on your private line."

"Sorry," I said. "I hope you can get to sleep now."

"I'll just take one of my sleeping pills," she replied.

I heard the door close and listened to my mother's footsteps retreating. I thought about all of her social causes. She either was or had been president of every women's organization in town, and last year she had been appointed to the governor's task force on the environment. It had been the biggest thrill of her life, and she traveled around the state, making speeches a couple of times a month. Most of the time I couldn't blame her for wanting to be involved in so many things since my dad's business keeps him away from home so much, but sometimes I wished she could just be around for me a little more often. Maybe then she'd get to know Drew and find out what a really great person he is.

Drew was on Mom's blacklist as it was. Thank goodness she didn't know that he had been in a drug rehab program for six weeks last summer. He had checked himself in. He had asked for help. These days, how many other seniors in high school could claim going through rehab? I thought. Lots! The hospitals had waiting lists as long as your arm, and sometimes it seemed as if kids thought going through rehab was the socially correct thing to do. It certainly was no disgrace. But Mom would never see it that way.

Still, Drew wasn't a user in the real sense. Never had been, for that matter. And the rehab program had been mostly to help him resist temptation. To help with Andy.

I shuddered, remembering Keeley's call. Drew needed me. Needed me *bad*. I had to go to him if I could.

There was no light shining under my door now,

and the only sound was the soft whir of the paddle fan overhead, gently moving the fragrant air, which was unusually warm and humid for a January night, even in southwest Florida. I got out of bed and tiptoed through the open sliding-glass doors and out onto the lanai. The shattered reflection of the moon lay like a thousand shimmering fish on the surface of the swimming pool. It was gorgeous, and I usually stopped to look at it, but tonight I quickly skirted the pool and went to the far side of the screen enclosure. If the moon was bright enough, I might be able to see if there was a light on inside the one-room house perched at the end of Keeley Strachan's family's boat dock on the next canal over from ours.

The neighborhood where both our family and the Strachans lived was a series of streets laid out like fingers of land, little peninsulas stretching into a canal system that led directly to the Gulf of Mexico. The houses were large, and pleasure boats were docked behind most of them, huge oceangoing yachts, tall-masted sailboats, and smaller powerboats hanging above the water on electric lifts. Standing on tiptoe, I looked past my father's sailboat with its riggings whining in the breeze and my own twenty-five-foot cruiser, *Mellow Time,* which had been a present from my father on my seventeenth birthday. I squinted to see through the tall coconut palms separating the houses across the canal, and on to the next waterway and the end of the Strachans' dock, where the windows of the dock house glowed softly. Drew was there, and it looked as if he was awake.

I stood still for a moment, listening again. There was nothing but the usual night sounds, the breeze rustling the palm fronds, a fish jumping in the canal, tiny gecko lizards chirping in the hibiscus. My eyes flickered toward the second-floor balcony where glass doors led into my parents' bedroom. All was quiet up there, too, and the light was off. Hopefully, Mom had taken her pill and gone to sleep.

I dashed back to my room, skinning off my sleepshirt as I went. I dressed quickly in the darkness, pulling on shorts and a tank top and slipping into my favorite canvas shoes. I felt around on the dresser for something to tie up my long dark hair, and then pressed an ear against the door to the hall, listening harder than ever.

Quiet. Nothing but beautiful, deep, ear-pounding quiet. Filling my lungs with air, I said a quick prayer, and moved into the main part of the house, blinking at the eerie brightness as I tiptoed across the huge game room with glass doors leading to the pool. Like most of the house, it was done almost entirely in white, white tile on the floor, white leather upholstery, white this, white that, which reflected the moonlight with midday brilliance.

On the side of the room opposite the pool was a mirrored bar. I hurried to it and ran my fingers across a lower section of the mirror until I felt a tiny metal catch that would open a small door. Behind the door was the control panel for the house's security system, which my parents had installed to use when my father was traveling around the world for his hydraulic engineering business. It would set sirens blaring both here and downtown at the security company's monitoring office the instant anyone tried to open a door or cut through the screen on the lanai, and police cars would be swarming on the street in a matter of minutes. But all I had to do was switch it off. I couldn't hesitate any longer. I had to go to Drew.

A moment later I was racing through the dew-soaked grass. The moon lit the way as I cut through neighbors' backyards and turned the corner onto Keeley's street. She must have seen me coming, because she stepped out of the shadows beside her house the moment I reached her driveway.

"He just turned out the lights," she whispered.

I glanced toward the dock house. It lay in darkness.

"I doubt if he's asleep yet," I whispered back. "I'll go down and knock."

"Do you want the key, just in case?"

I considered it a moment and then shook my head. "I don't want to go barging in if he doesn't want to talk to me. Sometimes he gets pretty defensive about Andy."

Keeley reached out and gave my hand a reassuring squeeze. "Okay. I'll go on back to bed and see you in the morning."

I watched her disappear into the shadows again and

heard the faint click of the door close behind her. Then I hurried down the dock and knocked, listening intently for sounds inside.

Nothing. No one was stirring. I tried to see in the window beside the door, but curtains were drawn over it.

Knocking more insistently, I called out, "Drew, it's me. Please let me in. I want to talk to you."

I listened again, but still there was no sound coming from inside. I leaned against the door and waited, staring down into the murky blackness of the canal and wrinkling my nose at the strong kelpy smell of low tide.

I don't know how long I stood there, hoping that Drew would let me in. Somehow I knew that he wasn't asleep. He was sitting inside, waiting, too. Waiting for me to leave him alone with Andy. After a while I gave up and headed dejectedly for home.

chapter

2

"His pickup was gone when I got up this morning,"
said Keeley the instant I jumped into her white Mus-
tang convertible the next day for the ride to school.
"I'm sure he was okay, though. He would have stayed
put if he was in real trouble."

I felt a surge of hope. I had lain awake the rest of
the night, talking to Drew in my mind. Reminding
him that he had to be strong. Of course, he hadn't been
able to hear me. And just because Keeley believed he
was okay didn't mean he really was.

I glanced at Keeley. "Always the optimist, aren't
you?"

A grin broke over Keeley's round, freckled face,
and the wind blew her reddish-blond bangs out of her
eyes as she pulled the convertible out of the driveway.
"Better than always the pessimist, right?"

"Right," I murmured. What would I do without Keeley? I wondered. She definitely was always the optimist, and that was what I needed at the moment.

Keeley's face turned suddenly serious. "What are you going to do?"

"I'm going to find him the minute we get to school, and we're going to go see Mrs. Rothlis. She'll know what to do. She always does. She can talk to him, maybe about going back to rehab or maybe about trying something new. I don't know. I just trust her to be able to help him."

"But what if he doesn't want to see her?" asked Keeley. "You know how he hates to talk about Andy."

I sighed. "I know. I'll think of something."

Keeley pulled the car into the seniors' section of the school parking lot and shut off the engine. "Good luck," she said, giving me a sympathetic smile.

I got my books out of the backseat and looked around for Drew. His dark blue pickup was parked in the end space of the same row Keeley had pulled into. I squinted and looked closer. Drew was sitting behind the wheel. Waiting for me, I hoped.

He saw me coming and smiled. I smiled back and broke into a run. He looked so good. I loved his blue-green eyes. And his light brown hair was cut a little longer than the current fad, but on him it looked great. The minute I got close enough I noticed that his eyes were clear.

Relieved, I opened the door on the passenger's side of the cab and climbed inside.

"Keeley called and told me you were in her boat house," I began, not sure what to say. "I came as fast as I could, and I knocked, but you must have already been asleep."

"Hey, it's okay," said Drew, his husky voice full of reassurance. "I didn't do anything. Honest. I just needed a little space."

"Was it Andy? Did he come back?"

A shadow crossed Drew's face. "He tried."

"But you didn't let him?" I asked, studying his face for a clue before he could answer.

Drew shook his head.

"Come on, we've got to see Mrs. Rothlis," I said. I opened the door and jumped out. When Drew didn't move, I called, "Come on. We need to talk to her, whether you want to or not. And right now." I slammed the door and started walking toward the school.

He didn't follow. I stopped and waited. Maybe he was just taking his time. I knew better. There were only three people he ever talked to about Andy. Me, and for a long time I was the only one, but now he talked to Keeley, and Greg Brolin, Keeley's boyfriend, as well. Sometimes we would take *Mellow Time* out to Sand Dollar, which is a tiny uninhabited island a few miles south in the Gulf of Mexico. We would beach the boat and sit on the warm sand for hours, just talking. Those were some of the greatest times of my life, but they were great times for Drew, too. I don't think he'd ever opened up and told anyone about Andy before.

But there were things that Keeley and Greg and I simply couldn't help Drew with. We cared enough, but we didn't know enough. That was why he needed to talk to Mrs. Rothlis. She was more than a school counselor. She was everybody's friend. Besides that, I had a special relationship with her, which Drew was very well aware of. I helped out in her office as a student aide, taking care of things she never got around to doing, such as filing, straightening up her messy bookshelves, things like that. I didn't have a class first hour, and I usually stopped by then. It was my study period. Since I'm a senior, I could have gotten a pass to come to school at the start of second period, but I liked coming early with everybody else. Besides, it gave me an extra few minutes with Keeley and Drew.

Most of all, I liked being around Mrs. Rothlis. She was so comfortable. Sometimes we talked about important things. I talked to her when I had problems at home, and I had even confided in her about Andy. We giggled over silly things, too. I heard endless stories about her cat, which she had named Dumpster because she found him scrounging for food in the trash behind a restaurant. But right now it wasn't Dumpster who was on my mind.

I whirled around and stomped back to the pickup. This time I went around to the driver's side. "Drew!" I shouted.

He gave me a sideways glance through the closed window. Then he shook his head.

"You have to!" I insisted. "You have to get help!" I could hear my voice rising with emotion. I took a deep breath, trying to regain control. "You know Mrs. Rothlis isn't like other people. She's special."

Drew opened the door and climbed down from the cab of the truck.

"Okay, okay," he said, holding up his hands in surrender. "But I won't go see her now. It's almost time for the bell. I'll make an appointment for last period when I have study hall. I'll do it for you, if it will make you happy."

"No, Drew, you'll do it for *you*," I insisted. "And for us."

We parted at the entrance to the corridor where the banks of senior lockers stood. His was at one end, and mine was at the other. Angry voices caught my attention. Across the hall from my locker April McCarthy and Devin West were going at it again. They fought all the time, and there were rumors that he hit her sometimes. Drew would never do a thing like that. He was sweet and wonderful and almost perfect, except for his problem with Andy, and I was going to see to it that he got help if it was the last thing I ever did.

I worked my combination, wondering if he would

clam up for Mrs. Rothlis. *But that's so stupid!* I almost said out loud. If there was anyone he could trust to give him advice about Andy besides the three of us, it was the counselor.

I leaned my forehead against the cool metal of the locker and thought about that moonlit night last spring, when Drew and I had taken *Mellow Time* out to Sand Dollar Island. We had played and splashed in the water for a while and then stretched out on our beach towels to talk. Before long, Drew was telling me about Andy.

"Andy's a little kid," he had begun. "He's eight, going on nine. His parents are big-deal yuppie lawyers, both of them. They're too, too cool, man. They drive twin BMWs and have a penthouse condo on the beach." Anger began creeping into his voice. "They bought in to the dream. They thought nothing could touch them. Boy, were they wrong."

He lapsed into silence, and I could see that he was in that other world.

"They started doing coke at parties. No big deal, right? Everybody was doing it. And it couldn't hurt you. It wasn't addictive. Everybody knew that. And man, it was fun! You know, it got to be so much fun that they started giving it to Andy. Not much. Just a little bit now and then. But, hey, every little kid's entitled to some fun, right?"

Drew's eyes were blazing. "And they thought it was fun watching Andy get high. And what did he know?

They were his parents, right? And they said it was okay."

Drew had paused, his face drawn with sorrow. "And pretty soon they quit going to work every day. It was more fun to stay home and do coke. But it was getting pretty expensive. The first things they lost were the twin BMWs. Then the condo. Then their law practice. And just about that time my grandmother found out what was going on. And she came and got me and brought me to live with her. She helped me get off the stuff, and she said she was going to change everything about me. Make everything new and fresh and better. She even quit calling me Andy. For a while she just called me Andrew, but finally she nicked it to Drew. 'No reminders of the bad old days,' she said."

"And what about your parents?" I had asked.

"I don't know. Gram tried to help them, but they didn't want any part of it. They liked what they were doing. Can you believe that?" He shrugged in amazement. "She finally lost track of them. They could be on the streets now, for all I know. Or dead."

The first bell rang, and I let the memory fade. I shut my locker door and headed for Mrs. Rothlis's office. I walked along slowly, almost getting run over in the crush of students heading for their classes. Drew would have had plenty of time to make his appointment with her by now.

The door to Judy Rothlis's office was always open,

unless she was having a private conversation with a student.

"Come on in," she said cordially when I peeked in. She had on a comfortable-looking beige suit that contrasted with her short, dark hair, which she kept styled in a blunt cut, and she was doing paper work at her desk. "As you can see, the clutter monster has struck again!" she said with a throaty laugh.

I dumped my books into the chair beside her desk and looked around the small, overcrowded office, made more cluttered, and at the same time homey, by the abundance of collectibles in the shape of cats. As soon as the students had found out that their new counselor had a cat, she had been inundated with cat figurines, cat wall hangings, cat everything.

"So, how are things going?" asked Mrs. Rothlis, without looking up.

"Fine," I said, and picked up a stack of folders, heading for the cluster of file cabinets in one corner of the office.

"Oh, say, I saw your mother's picture in the paper earlier this week. Something about going to Tallahassee to meet with the governor about environmental issues," said the counselor.

I nodded. "It's that task force she's on. She's leaving tomorrow, and she'll be gone a few days," I said.

"Something's up," said Mrs. Rothlis. She had stopped working and was studying me closely.

"There's nothing wrong," I insisted, looking down at a clear glass paperweight in the shape of a cat that sat on the corner of her desk. I picked it up and rolled it from one hand to the other, feeling its smooth coolness and measuring its surprising heaviness before I spoke again. "I was just wondering if Drew Jansen came in to set up an appointment with you for later today."

Mrs. Rothlis nodded. "He stopped in before school. I set it up for last period today, which he said is his free period."

"He's coming to see you about Andy," I said. "He needs help again. I know he went through rehab last summer, but he still can't handle it by himself."

She looked pensive for a moment and then smiled reassuringly. "There are lots of alternatives out there. Don't worry, Ashlyn. He's going to be fine."

"Thanks," I murmured, replacing the cat paperweight on her desk. I opened the file drawer and tried to concentrate on stuffing the folders into their proper places, feeling such a mixture of relief and gratitude to Mrs. Rothlis that I could scarcely breathe.

I glanced up at a soft knock at the door. April McCarthy stuck her head in at Mrs. Rothlis's "Come in." But when April saw me, she started to duck back out again.

"April, don't leave," Mrs. Rothlis insisted. "Ashlyn is just doing a little work for me. I'm sure she'll excuse us if you'd like to talk in private."

"Sure, I can do this later," I said, and the counselor gave me an appreciative smile.

This sort of thing happened every once in a while, and I quickly picked up my books and headed out the door. As I passed April I couldn't help noticing that her eyes were red. She had definitely been crying. Probably about Devin. *Poor April,* I thought, *stuck with a jerk like that.*

My heart filled with gratitude again. I was a lot luckier than April. Drew was going to talk to Mrs. Rothlis last period. Everything was finally going to be okay.

chapter

3

I worried about Drew all morning, barely hearing what went on in my classes. What if he chickened out?

No, that's not fair, I reminded myself. There was nothing chicken about Drew. The problem was that he thought he was Superman. That he could handle it. He was determined to prove—mostly to himself—that he could beat Andy without anyone else's help. And that was what I had tried to tell him all along. That it was okay to ask for help.

Keeley and I have the same lunch period and usually go off campus to eat, but today she was making up a French test and so I grabbed a tuna sandwich and iced tea in the cafeteria, ate about half of it, and wandered out into the courtyard to get some sun and think about Drew. The only other kids out there were April and Devin. They quit talking when I walked past, but I could see that Devin was really steamed about something.

I went through the rest of the day like a zombie. I could hardly keep up with what was going on around me, as if I were operating on a thirty-second time delay behind the rest of the world. When the bell rang signaling the start of last period, all I could do was sit at my desk and try to picture what was going on in Mrs. Rothlis's office.

Was she gaining his confidence? Was he telling her about Andy? What if he closed himself off again and refused her help?

Drew's pickup was gone from the parking lot when Keeley and I got there after school.

Keeley must have sensed my tension, because her freckled face brightened and she said, "Looks like they finished early. I'll bet it was a good session or they would still be at it."

I shook my head in amazement. "How can you always be so upbeat about everything?"

"Oh, you know, I have great parents who spoil me rotten, a fabulous home life, and a dog," she teased.

I couldn't help laughing. It was our usual routine. Keeley always blamed my problems on the fact that my father was always away on some engineering project, and my mother was too busy with her clubs and charities to spend any time with me. She said the worst part was, Mom wouldn't let me have a pet. We carried it to extremes sometimes, but it never failed to raise my spirits.

"Want to go to the mall?" she asked, easing the car into traffic. "I hear Berg's is having a sale."

"Naw," I said. Already my spirits were doing a nose dive again. "I think if you don't mind I'll just go on home and wait for Drew to call."

No one was home when Keeley dropped me off. Mom was off doing heaven only knew what, and Greta was already gone for the day. I automatically sniffed the air to try to figure out by aroma alone what she had fixed for our supper. Today it definitely smelled Italian. Greta worked for us from eight thirty in the morning until four in the afternoon, except when both of my parents were away. Then she moved into the smallest guest bedroom and stayed around the clock. She had worked for us for as long as I could remember, and I loved her company and the way she hummed John Philips Sousa marches while she worked.

But for now the house was empty and silent. Too silent. Come on, telephone, ring.

I prowled from room to room, too restless to concentrate on homework or go for a swim. I wasn't even hungry, although Greta had left a plate of warm peanut butter cookies on the kitchen counter.

Why didn't Drew call? It was almost five o'clock and I was starting to get angry. Classes had been out for the day since ten after three, and he had been supposed to see Mrs. Rothlis during last period. Had something gone wrong?

I drummed my fingers on the phone in my room. He didn't work at the marina today, so he was probably home by now. Should I call there? I decided against it. It wouldn't do any good. He would never talk about Andy in front of his grandmother.

I wandered into the kitchen again and took a cookie off the plate. As I took a nibble, I heard the soft hum of the garage door opening. Mom was home.

A car door slammed in the garage, and a moment later she entered the kitchen. She barely gave me a glance as she headed straight for the stairs. I supposed that she had a lot on her mind. Even for her, meeting the governor was a big deal.

"I'm going up to finish my packing," she called over her shoulder. Just before she reached the stairway she stopped and slowly turned around. "I'm sorry, dear. I didn't mean to ignore you." She was smiling apologetically. "Did you have a good day?"

It was obvious that anything to do with me or my day was nothing more than an afterthought to her, as usual. She had much more important things on her mind.

"Yeah, it was super," I lied.

"That's nice," she said. "I hope you won't mind eating alone tonight. It's going to take me all evening to get ready for my trip. I'm sure Greta left something in the refrigerator."

I watched her turn again and go up the steps, thinking that it probably wasn't so strange that we were usually on different wavelengths. Our personalities were nothing alike, and besides that, we couldn't be more different in appearance. She was tall, thin, and stunningly beautiful. I had stopped growing at five feet two in eighth grade, and I had to keep a constant watch on my waistline. My hair was dark brown and wavy. Hers was champagne-blond and piled high on her head. I had no idea what color her roots were. She was careful never to let them show. Even our eyes were different colors. Mine were brown, like my father's. Hers were a pale blue.

The shrill sound of the phone caught me by surprise. It was my private line, and I dashed for my room, grabbing it before it could ring again.

"Hello?"

"Ashlyn! I've got to talk to you! Something awful's happened!"

It was Drew and he sounded scared.

"What is it?" I cried.

"I . . . I can't tell you over the phone. You've got to meet me. Now. Somewhere. Anywhere."

"Are you okay?" My voice was reduced to a squeak as I tried to control my panic.

"Yes. Just meet me!"

"Okay. Where?"

I could hear his ragged breathing as he tried to think. I was thinking, too.

"Keeley's dock house!" I shouted. "She's gone to the mall, and no one else will be home at this hour. You know where the key is hidden."

"Okay," he said breathlessly. "And hurry, Ashlyn, just hurry."

I raced out of my room and through the house, not stopping to get the keys to any of the cars. I could get there faster on foot. Besides, I didn't want Mom to know I was gone. From the sound of Drew's voice, this was something major.

"Oh, please don't let it be Andy," I murmured over and over again as I ran. But I knew it could be anything. Had he been in an accident?

Drew was standing in the open door to the dock house when I got there. His face was a ghastly white.

I pushed him inside and shut the door behind us. Dim light came through the windows of the single room, which served as an overflow guest room to the main house.

Drew staggered across the room and sank onto the sofa, burying his head in his hands.

"What is it?" I demanded. "Drew, tell me. What happened?"

He looked up into my face and began sobbing. "I didn't do it. She was already dead when I got there. Oh, Ashlyn, you've got to believe me. I didn't kill Mrs. Rothlis!"

Shock rolled over me, distorting his words and making his voice sound like a tape played at the wrong speed. Surely I had misunderstood. My eyes searched his face for confirmation.

Surely he hadn't said that Mrs. Rothlis was dead.

chapter

4

It was a long time before the buzzing in my head stopped. A longer time before Drew's words made sense. Mrs. Rothlis was dead. Murdered.

A part of me wondered why I didn't cry or scream or let my emotions out, but I guess I was still too stunned to believe it. Too much in shock to feel the pain.

"I skipped my appointment with her last period," he began, once he had gotten hold of himself. "I just couldn't go. I kept thinking that I need to handle Andy myself. He's part of me, for God's sake! If I can't get rid of him, nobody can.

"Anyway, I hung around in the hall near her office door for a few minutes after the bell rang for last period, talking myself out of going to see her, and then left school. I hated myself for doing it, but I couldn't help it. I had to. I drove around. I don't even know where I went. All I could do was think about Andy. And about the mess my life was in. And I thought about Gram and how she'd feel if she knew Andy was still around. And I thought about you and the promise I had made to get help. That was when I decided to go back. I still didn't have much faith that she could do anything, but it was worth a try. I'd tell her I was sorry I'd skipped out and hear what she had to say.

"By then school had been out for more than an hour, but I knew Mrs. Rothlis stayed late sometimes. I decided to check, and her car was still in the parking lot."

He paused, looking at me with fright-filled eyes.

"Go on," I whispered, dreading what he was about to say. There was a terrible ache building in my chest, and my head felt as if it would explode.

He nodded and reached for my hand. "The door to her office was pulled to, but it wasn't latched. When I knocked, it opened slightly, and I could see that no one was sitting in the chair in front of her desk. I knew that if she was in there, she was alone."

He paused again, swallowing hard at the memory of what came next.

"I pushed it open a little farther and called her name. That's when I saw her. She was lying on the floor, just sort of crumpled up. Her eyes were closed. There was this big purple gash on her forehead, and blood was splattered everywhere." Drew buried his face in his hands and sobbed. "Ashlyn, she was dead! I knew it as soon as I saw her."

"Are you *sure*, Drew?" I cried, hoping against hope that he was mistaken. "Maybe she *wasn't* dead! Did you check her pulse?"

"Yeah, I checked it—at least a dozen times. And I tried to remember the CPR I learned for my lifeguard test. I don't know if I got it right, but I tried. Ashlyn, you've got to believe me. I really *tried!*"

"What did you do then? Did you call nine-one-one?" I pleaded, still hoping that somehow everything had worked out and that she was alive and okay right now.

Drew shook his head. "I started to. I even went to her desk and picked up the phone. Then I freaked. I heard somebody out in the hall. I looked through the crack in the door and saw one of the custodians a few doors down, cleaning up. He was moving toward her office. When he looked the other direction, I bolted. I don't think he saw me. But I know he called nine-one-one, because I parked a block away and watched the school. The emergency truck got there in a couple of minutes. I didn't stick around to see them bring her out, though. I just couldn't."

"Drew, listen to me," I said. My voice crackled with emotion, and I sucked in a breath to stop it. I had to stay in control for Drew's sake until later when I was alone. "It was probably an accident. Maybe she fell and hit her head—on—on—on the corner of her desk."

Drew looked up slowly, shaking his head. His eyes were deadly serious. "She was too far away from the desk. Over by the file cabinets. Ashlyn, somebody killed her. Somebody murdered Mrs. Rothlis. And it must have happened just before I got there."

Suddenly I felt anger flare. This time I couldn't hold my emotions in, and I stood up and stomped around the dock house, waving my arms as I talked. "But who, Drew? Who? You know as well as I do that everybody loved her. She didn't have an enemy in the world. Nobody would want to hurt her, much less *kill* her."

"I know, I know," Drew murmured, shaking his head. "It must have been something bizarre, like she walked in on a drug deal or something. That's why I had to get out of there. Somebody might think I killed her."

"You!" I exploded. "Why would anybody think a thing like that?"

He lowered his eyes, looking away fearfully. "Get serious. You know as well as I do that a lot of people know I've been in rehab, and if someone told the police I'd be dead meat. They would think up all sorts of scenarios about me skipping out on the appointment and then coming back high, me going berserk, you know the stuff I mean. They'd nail me."

I closed my eyes and let out a long, slow breath.
Drew was right, of course. Everyone would just assume
that because he'd had trouble with drugs before, he was
a junkie now.

"Maybe they won't find out," I offered.

Drew shook his head, his jaw muscles working.
"Don't count on it. Things have a way of getting out.
Rumors start. And the police have ways of digging up
stuff. Stuff about my parents. About my rehab. Don't
you see? I couldn't take a chance."

Neither of us said anything for a long time. We just
sat there, holding each other, and playing the awful
possibilities over and over in our minds.

"Look, let's both go home. Act like nothing's happened. And wait to see what comes on the news," I
suggested after a while. "Maybe she *isn't* dead. Or
maybe the police already know who did it."

We left the dock house hand in hand and said
good-bye at Drew's truck, which was parked in front of
the main house. No one was home at the Strachans'
yet. I couldn't stand to think about Keeley, happily
shopping at the mall, oblivious to all that was going on.

It wasn't until I was back in the quiet house, in my
own room with the door closed, that I began to trem-
ble. At first only my hands were shaking. Then tremors
started to build, racking my body and setting my teeth
clacking against each other, until it was as if a volcano
had erupted inside me. Then came the flood of tears.

Mrs. Rothlis was dead. Killed. By someone who didn't know how special she was. How caring.

I could feel a cry gathering in my throat. I wanted to let it out, but I knew I couldn't make a sound. Not now, with my mother in the room above mine, packing for her trip. I had to hold it in until in the morning when she was gone and pretend nothing had happened or else risk jeopardizing Drew.

I stayed in my room all evening. I knew Mom wouldn't think anything was wrong. She was too busy. In the morning she would be off, hobnobbing with the governor.

At eleven P.M. the local newscast came on TV. I had my own small color set, which sat on the edge of my dresser. At one minute until eleven, I clicked on the remote. I would find out for myself if this was really happening or if it was just some horrible nightmare.

I was too antsy to sit down, so I stood in front of the set and watched in a trance as the perky fresh-from-college nighttime anchorwoman's smiling face filled the screen. It seemed incredible that she could smile that way, her bouncy blond curls brushing her shoulders, and at the same time announce that a popular school counselor had been found murdered at a local high school.

"Details on this and other stories, right after these messages," she said, and then her face faded away, leaving only the image of her Cheshire-cat smile in my mind while the commercials blurred by.

"Thanks for joining us tonight," said the smiling anchorwoman. "Now for tonight's top story. Authorities were called to Quentin Sargeant High School late this afternoon when a custodian discovered the body of thirty-eight-year-old Judith Rothlis, a first-year guidance counselor at the school. According to police, Rothlis was found in her office. She apparently died from a single blow to her right temple. No motive has been established for the murder, and employees at the school are in a state of shock."

The picture cut away to a scene at the school. I shook my head in disbelief as I saw that Mr. Claxton, one of the custodians, was about to be interviewed. He was standing in the hall outside Mrs. Rothlis's office door, where yellow crime-scene tape was stretched to prevent the public from going inside. Behind him I could see several plainclothes policemen moving around in the office. There were a couple of uniformed policemen, and a third man wearing a dark suit who was bending over a spot on the floor.

Mr. Claxton wiped away tears with the back of his hand and said, "I can't believe it. Who would do a thing like this? Everybody liked her. *Everybody*."

Mr. Claxton disappeared from the screen, and the anchorwoman reappeared.

"In other news, a semitrailer overturned near the intersection . . ."

I shut out the sight and sounds of the television as I felt the cry I had suppressed earlier gathering in my throat again. This time I couldn't hold it back.

A moment later the door burst open, and Mom rushed into the room. "Ashlyn, what's wrong? Are you all right?"

I felt my face crumple and heard little whimpers coming from myself. I didn't want her to see me that way, but I couldn't help it. "It's Mrs. Rothlis. It was on the news. She's dead."

My mother looked at me with a blank expression.

"You know. The counselor. The one I work for as a student aide. She's been murdered."

I buried my face in my hands and felt Mom's arms slip around my shoulders.

"I'm sorry, sweetheart," she said gently. "I think I did hear something about it on the news a few minutes ago. I guess I was just so preoccupied with my trip that I didn't make the connection."

She stroked my hair while I blew my nose. I knew I must look awful, but for once she didn't say anything about it.

"Ashlyn, you're so upset, why don't you take one of my sleeping pills? That way you'll feel better in the morning."

"No, thanks. I'll be okay. Don't worry."

Mom nodded and then said good-night. I watched her go, thinking how amazing it was she didn't understand that it wasn't a sleeping pill I needed. I needed her.

Why does she have to go away just when I need her? I wondered. *Why does it always happen that way?*

chapter

5

It's hard to explain why Mrs. Rothlis meant so much to me. I lay awake most of the night thinking about it and remembering the day we met. It was only a couple of weeks after school started, and I stopped by her office to get information on some colleges I was interested in. I had expected to find a dignified faculty person sitting behind the desk, but I was in for a surprise. She had pushed a chair to the wall of books opposite her desk to use as a step stool, and there she was, in her bare feet, stretched all the way up to the top shelf, raking books onto the floor with a ruler.

She looked so funny that I burst out laughing.

"Oh, dear. I didn't know I had a visitor. Come on in," she said as she got down off the chair and tried to regain some dignity. "I'm Mrs. Rothlis. Is there something I can do for you?"

"Hi," I said, still chuckling. "I was just looking for some college information, but I can come back later if you're busy."

The counselor glanced at the mess on the floor and then gave me a big smile. "It's nothing that can't wait. Actually, the former counselor left the filing system in such a mess that I can't find a thing. I thought if I got things down where I could see them, I might have better luck. I think these are college catalogs I just pushed onto the floor, as a matter of fact."

I liked her instantly. She was my kind of person. Not stuffy and rigid like a lot of people. My mother, to name one.

She plopped down on the floor and began sorting through the pamphlets and books. I dropped to my knees beside her, and we kept up a steady stream of conversation while we sorted through them together. By the time we found what I had asked for, we had discovered that we both liked Mexican food, cats, and Gilbert and Sullivan. A few days later she asked me to be her student aide.

One of the things I liked best about Mrs. Rothlis was that she always liked me just the way I was. That's a real contrast to my mother. I know she means well, but Mom criticizes me about every little thing. For instance, she hates the way I wear my hair. She says I would look better in a style that's more classical and not so faddish. Mrs. Rothlis liked my hair. She said it looked like something right out of a magazine.

That's just one thing. I could go on and on. Like Mom's opinion of Drew. He works after school three afternoons a week at a local marina as a boat mechanic. He said he liked working with his hands. Of course Mom looks down her nose at that.

"I can't understand why Camille Jansen allows that grandson of hers to work as a *boat mechanic,*" she had said a few weeks back. "She's a dear, sweet person, but you'd think that she would want him to do something more in keeping with their social status. After all, Camille is the wealthiest woman in town."

I had tuned out the rest of her commentary. I already knew the story of Mrs. Jansen's father, Quentin Sargeant, who had bought up thousands of acres of land in the days when nobody thought the southwest coast of Florida was good for anything except raising alligators and mosquitoes. But Quentin Sargeant had been a man of vision, as the old saying goes, and the shores of the Gulf of Mexico now sported golf courses, marinas, and high-rise condominiums that he had developed. Even the local high school bore Quentin Sargeant's name. Still, Drew's grandmother didn't flaunt her money. She didn't hobnob with the social bigwigs.

I knew that was part of what puzzled my mother. Mom loved the finer things of life, as she put it. The country club was her second home, and being chosen by the governor for his environmental task force had made her ecstatic. It was beyond her comprehension why anyone who had the kind of money Mrs. Jansen had would avoid social gatherings like the plague, much less allow her only grandchild to get his hands dirty repairing boat engines.

The other thing that bothered Mom was the secrecy that surrounded Drew's coming to live with his grandmother when he was ten years old. Camille never mentioned her only child, Quentin Jansen, and his wife Darcy, who were Drew's parents, or what had happened after they went to Miami to open their own law practice. All anyone knew was that after a while Drew had suddenly come to live with his grandmother. Lots of local busybodies had tried to find out about Quent and Darcy, but there were no records anywhere. It was as if they had never existed.

Mom didn't know that Drew had confided the whole story to me.

I had complained once to my dad about how picky Mom was, and he had said that she simply had high standards. He said she was proud of her social position and her accomplishments and that she wanted the same kind of life for me. That's not so bad, I guess, but I just wish she'd let me choose for myself.

All those things churned through my mind as I tossed and turned, but something else kept me awake, too. Something that happened last Tuesday.

I was working on a special project for Mrs. Rothlis. She had asked me to rearrange her bookshelves, putting the reference books into subject categories. They had been shelved alphabetically by author before. I had almost completed the change on Tuesday morning, so, since I needed only a few minutes to finish up, I stopped in her office after school.

"Ashlyn, I've got a great idea," said Mrs. Rothlis the minute I put the last book into its proper slot on the shelf. "I know what a boring job this has been for you, and it means so much to me to have everything arranged so I can find it, so why don't you come home with me right now, and we'll have a little victory celebration. Nothing fancy. Just a cup of tea. When we're finished, I'll run you home. How about it?"

I hesitated, not because I didn't want to go, but because I'd never thought about going to the home of any of my teachers or counselors.

Mrs. Rothlis flashed a smile. "I'll introduce you to Dumpster," she offered.

"It's a deal," I said, returning her smile.

The air coming in the open window of Mrs. Rothlis's old Chevy van got hotter and more sticky as we moved inland, away from the cool Gulf breezes. The homes were smaller in this part of town, and instead of posh high-rise condos with ocean views, the apartment complexes were modest and built close to the ground. Still, I felt unexpectedly at home when she opened the door of her tiny second-floor walk-up apartment and ushered me in.

"Look out for Dumpster," she called out cheerfully

as I stepped into the dusky living room, where the window shades had been left closed against the afternoon sun.

Suddenly something whizzed out of a dark corner and brushed against my legs, disappearing into the shadows on the other side of the room.

Mrs. Rothlis laughed as she opened one of the shades, exposing the soft greens and pinks of the upholstered furniture to the light. "Whoops! You've already met him. He gets lonesome, being alone all day, and he's always so glad for company that he zips around like Road Runner when I first get home from school."

I loved it. Mom would never let me have a pet. She said they smelled, and left unwelcome deposits on the carpet. She would absolutely freak over a cat like Dumpster. "Here Dumpster! Here, kitty, kitty," I coaxed.

This time the gray-and-white cat jumped off a bookcase and streaked under the sofa, again softly grazing my legs.

"He likes you. That's why he's brushing against you," said Mrs. Rothlis. "Make space for yourself on the sofa while I fix us some tea, and he'll be in your lap in a second."

I pushed aside the stacks of books that almost covered the shabby, overstuffed green sofa and sat down, looking around the apartment while the counselor puttered in her tiny efficiency kitchen, putting on the teakettle. Even though it was small, it was a warm and comfortable home, stuffed with unpretentious furniture and mounds of greenery and hanging plants.

About a year ago I had gotten rid of all the white furniture Mom had picked out for my room and redecorated with rattan furniture, jungle prints on the bedspread and chairs, and all the potted palms and ferns that I could crowd in. Mom had given me a quick smile and said that it was beautiful, but deep down I knew she hated it. She loves white—white walls, white tile floors, white furniture with splashes of color for accent. She calls it pure, and clean, and regal. To me it's boring. I love the overgrown-jungle look, and I even bought a stuffed gorilla that I called Tarzan to hang in one palm tree and a carved wooden snake I named Fang to lie at the foot of my bed. But now, standing in Mrs. Rothlis's apartment, I was struck by how much our decorating tastes were alike.

Suddenly Dumpster appeared airborne from over my left shoulder and landed in my lap, purring as loudly as a jet airplane.

"See, what did I tell you? He loves you already."

Mrs. Rothlis teetered into the room, a mug of tea, filled practically to overflowing, in each hand. "I'd never make a waitress," she said, sloshing liquid over the side as she set mine on the glass-topped coffee table in front of me.

"Me, either," I confessed. "I'm a total klutz. Do

you remember the old saying, can't walk and chew gum at the same time? Well, I'm the one who inspired it."

The counselor settled into a deep-cushioned chair opposite me. Her throaty laughter was irresistible, and instantly I was laughing along with her.

"I propose a toast to a job well done," she said, raising her mug in the air.

"I'll drink to that!" I added, raising my mug, too.

We sipped our tea and made small talk while Dumpster entertained us by zipping around the room again. Once he disappeared briefly, only to return carrying a wadded-up sock in his mouth.

Mrs. Rothlis looked embarrassed for a moment. Then she burst out laughing. "Dumpster!" she scolded. "How many times have I told you to leave my tennis socks in my sneakers." Looking at me, she added, "He never does that when we're alone, just when I have company."

That set us laughing again. I loved it. It was so cool to be there with her, talking, laughing. I couldn't remember when I'd felt so at home. In fact, I wished the afternoon would never end.

"So, Ashlyn, while we're getting better acquainted, why not tell me something about your family? Start at the beginning," she suggested.

"At the beginning?" I asked in surprise.

"Sure. Why not? Tell me where you were born, for instance," she said with a casual wave of her hand.

I shrugged. "Okay." Then I chuckled. "Well, actually I wasn't born in Florida, even though I've lived here all my life. I was born in Chicago. My dad was just starting his hydraulic engineering business, and he was overseas—Morocco, I think—and Mom went home to her parents to have me."

"And she brought you back to Florida when your dad came home?" asked the counselor.

"Right. I was five months old then, and I've been here ever since. Same house, and everything. Pretty boring stuff, huh?"

"Only if you think so. Looks pretty idyllic to me. Wealthy family. Gorgeous home on the water. Even your own boat. Wow!" she exclaimed softly.

"Yeah, well . . ." I sighed. "Looks aren't everything. I get lonely sometimes. Mom's busy with her causes, and Dad's away so much. He works mostly in the deserts overseas. He's in Egypt right now."

"And when he's home, do you do things together?"

"Yes, sort of." I struggled to explain. "I mean, he tries, but he's been gone so much that he can't really relate to my life. I know he wants to. I guess it's just hard."

"I'm really impressed with your mother," she said, gazing into her tea and running a finger around the lip of the mug. "Working with the governor is quite an honor."

"Yeah," I said, feeling a surge of pride. "She's really

involved in environmental issues. She works for a bunch of other causes, too. She believes that since we're—well, you know—pretty well-off, we should do everything we can to help others."

"That's very commendable," said the counselor. She took a sip of tea and stared silently into the dark liquid as if she were thinking over Mom's philosophy of life.

The ring of the telephone startled both of us, and Mrs. Rothlis excused herself and went into the tiny kitchen, taking the receiver from the phone on the wall.

"Hello? Oh, yes, I'm glad you called."

She listened for a moment and then spoke again in confidential tones. "I'm almost positive I was right. I think I've finally found—"

She broke off, glancing quickly at me. I looked away, embarrassed. I hadn't meant to listen in on her private call.

"I can't talk now. I have company. I'll call you later."

"Nothing important," she said, dismissing the call with a wave of her hand when she sat down again. "Now, where were we?"

It was getting late, so I stayed only a few minutes longer. I gave Dumpster a good-bye hug, and then Mrs. Rothlis drove me home. Naturally we found things to laugh about all the way.

Now, as I watched dawn paint the sky outside my bedroom window a brilliant salmon-pink, I longed to have that Tuesday afternoon back again. I couldn't believe that she was dead, when just last week we had started to become such good friends.

chapter

6

The phone rang while I was getting dressed the next
morning.

"Ashlyn, did you hear about Mrs. Rothlis?" Keeley
shrieked when I mumbled hello. "She's dead!"

I sank slowly onto the bed, perching on the edge
and clutching the phone as tears welled up again. "I
know," I finally managed to say. I felt a stab of guilt for
not calling Keeley last night and telling her about the
counselor's death myself. After all, she was my best
friend. But somehow last night I hadn't been able to
talk about it even to her.

"Turn on the TV," Keeley urged. "They're talking
about it right now on Channel Six."

"Hold on," I said. I threw down the phone and
raced around the end of my bed, punching the television on. It was already set to Channel Six.

Instantly a silver-haired man with a mustache appeared at the news desk. "Homicide investigators at the scene say a witness saw a young man, possibly a student, hurrying away from the school shortly before the murder was discovered. The suspect reportedly drove away in a dark blue pickup truck. The investigation will continue today. In other news . . ."

I stared at the screen, no longer seeing the reporter or hearing what he was saying. All I could think about was Drew. *Someone had seen him!*

I spun around as a piercing whistle filled the air. "Hey, Ashlyn! Are you still there?" a tiny voice cried.

I grabbed the receiver off the bed. "Gosh, Keeley, I forgot you were still on the phone."

"Did you hear what they said about the pickup?" Keeley asked gravely. "They said it was dark blue. Ashlyn, Drew has a dark blue pickup."

"Oh, Keeley, I know. I've got to talk to you. How soon can you get here?"

"Was it Drew's pickup? He isn't in trouble, is he?"

I took a deep breath and let it out slowly. "I don't think he's in trouble. But hurry. I need to talk to you anyway."

As soon as Keeley hung up I tried to call Drew, but the phone rang and rang.

"Come on, Drew, Mrs. Jansen. Please, somebody answer!" I pleaded, but after the fifteenth ring I hung up.

Don't panic, I told myself angrily. *Drew needs me, and there's probably a simple explanation for why neither he nor his grandmother is home at this hour of the morning.* But I couldn't think of a single one.

My mother had left for the airport before I got up, and I suppose she didn't come in to tell me good-bye because she thought I was asleep. That was okay. I wasn't up to facing conversation about Mrs. Rothlis's murder at that hour, and even though I was waiting in the driveway when Keeley pulled up for the ride to school, I wasn't feeling much better. Still, I knew that if I didn't talk to someone pretty soon, I'd explode.

"I just can't believe it, Ashlyn. Who would do such a thing?" Keeley blurted out the instant I got into the car. "*Nobody* would ever want to hurt Mrs. Rothlis. It just doesn't make any sense." Then she grew silent, turning to look at me with troubled eyes. "What about Drew? He didn't have anything to do with it, did he?"

I shook my head. "No, at least not exactly. Let's get out of here and go somewhere we can talk."

"Right," said Keeley.

She pulled the convertible out of the driveway and quickly left the neighborhood, turning north. I knew she was heading to the beach. Neither of us spoke as we searched the palm-lined streets for a parking space.

January is the peak tourist season in Florida, but in spite of the large number of cars parked on the streets leading to the beach, the long stretch of white sand was relatively uncrowded. Keeley and I headed toward the water. We passed the long wooden fishing pier jutting out into the water and walked along slowly, leaving footprints in the smooth band of sand between where the soft waves brushed the shore and the shell-strewn tide line above. Overhead a flock of laughing gulls lived up to their name.

After a while we stopped. Keeley sat down in the sand and looked up at me expectantly.

"Okay, now you can tell me about Drew," she urged gently.

I squatted down beside her, playing with the sand beside my knee and squinting out to sea before answering, watching a sailboat glide across the smooth waters of the Gulf. The sun shone on the water with painful brilliance. I had the awful feeling that I was betraying Drew. And yet Drew had trusted Keeley to know about Andy. Surely he would trust her now, too.

"Drew was the one who found her, but he panicked and ran," I said, opening my hand and letting sand slip away between my fingers. I went on to explain about how he had skipped his appointment and then, feeling guilty, had gone back an hour after school let out and had found Mrs. Rothlis's body. "When he realized she was dead, he just freaked."

Keeley's gaze had been fixed out over the calm sea while I spoke, as if her mind was a million miles away. Now she turned to me and murmured, "And somebody saw him and told the police. Poor Drew." She shook her head in disbelief. "Everyone in school knows him and knows he has a dark blue pickup, so it's just a matter of time before the witness will identify him."

"If he hasn't already," I said. "I tried to call his house, but no one answered. It scares me to think that his grandmother wasn't home so early in the morning. I just hope everything's okay."

I glanced at my watch. "Oh, my gosh. If we don't hurry, we'll be late for school. And who knows, maybe I'm worrying for nothing. Maybe Drew's already there, waiting for me."

I started to leave, but Keeley hesitated.

"Ashlyn, before we go I just want you to know how sorry I am about Mrs. Rothlis. I know how special she was to you. I liked her, too, but it wasn't the same. It was almost as if she picked you out at the beginning of the year and made a special project of being your friend."

I nodded. "She hardly knew me when she chose me to be her student aide. I don't know how I got so lucky. And now she's gone." I shook my head in wonder. "I just can't believe that she's really dead."

Drew's truck wasn't in the parking lot when we got to school, so I walked toward the building with Keeley, determined to stay cool until I knew for sure where he was. A crowd of students had gathered near the front entrance where a uniformed policeman stood, arms crossed in front and jaw set firmly.

Most of the students were silent, staring first at the officer and then at the yellow crime-scene tape strung across the closed front door. I stared at the door, seeing inside in my mind. Quentin Sargeant High School was laid out in a huge one-story rectangle that covered most of a city block. Classrooms formed the long sides of the rectangle, with doors on either side of each room, one opening into a hallway and the other opening into a center courtyard. Students congregated under palm trees or on small benches in the courtyard at noon and before the morning bell. The small part of the rectangle at the far end of the building housed the gymnasium and cafeteria. The section at the front of the school where we stood now was where the offices were located, those of the principal, assistant principal, school nurse, and the counselor, as well as the library.

In my mind I traveled in the front door, past the office, past the glass trophy case in the center of the foyer, and on to the second door on the left. I could see the name plate on the open door, MRS. JUDITH ROTHLIS, COUNSELOR, the clutter of cat memorabilia on the walls and bookshelves. I strained to see the desk and the person sitting behind it, but I couldn't. It wouldn't come into focus. I blinked, feeling as if I were looking through fog, but the blur wouldn't clear.

Gradually I became aware of bits of conversation in the crowd around me, spoken mostly in soft, reverent tones.

"She was the nicest person in the whole school."

"Yeah, I can't believe it. This kind of thing happens somewhere else, not here."

"Who do you think did it?"

"Probably some druggie."

My ears pricked at the word "druggie." But just then there was a stirring in the crowd. I glanced toward where the sound was loudest. Mrs. Sandel, the school principal, was making her way among the groups of students and heading toward the front door. She stopped beside the police officer, spoke to him for a moment, and turned to face us. Her silver hair caught the glint of morning sunlight, and her usually stern face was creased with sadness.

All whispers stopped, and she spoke without needing to raise her voice to be heard.

"Students, on this tragic morning I would like all of you to go to the gymnasium for a short assembly before passing to your first-period classes. Thank you."

Like sleepwalkers, the student body filed silently around the side of the school and into the courtyard through an opening between two classrooms. From there we headed for the gym at the far end.

I was still searching the crowd for Drew. He wasn't with Greg Brolin, or with Tipp Ludwig or Jake Copland, two friends who worked with him at the marina.

Naturally Keeley made a beeline for Greg, and when we got near I whispered to him, "Have you seen Drew?"

Greg shook his head and shrugged. "I just got here, and I didn't see his truck in the lot."

I looked away so that neither of them would see the worry on my face. Something was definitely wrong. Drew was almost never late for school. His grandmother was strict about punctuality. She would never let him oversleep—as if he could sleep after what happened yesterday.

We found seats halfway up the bleachers, and I continued watching for Drew among the students streaming in the door until it was closed behind the last few stragglers and Mrs. Sandel stepped behind the podium in the center of the stage. Beside her was the policeman who had been stationed by the front door a few minutes ago and a somber man in a dark suit and tie. Two other policemen had come into the gym and were standing near the exits.

Mrs. Sandel raised her hand to shush the murmurs that were beginning to build across the room. "Students, may I have your attention, please?"

The gym grew quiet again, and she went on. "As I'm sure you are all aware by now, our counselor, Mrs. Judith Rothlis, died yesterday afternoon. We on the faculty are all deeply moved and saddened by this tragedy, just as you students are. We think that it is important to maintain as normal a school schedule as possible. Of course, any of you who wish to attend the funeral will be excused at that time.

"This afternoon a crisis team will arrive from the Ft. Myers school district. The three-member team will be available to any of you who would like to talk to someone about what you're feeling. They will stay at Quentin Sargeant as long as they're needed, and I'd like to urge any of you who feel the need to seek them out."

I stared into my lap as I listened to Mrs. Sandel. I could never talk to strangers about Mrs. Rothlis or how I felt about her when she was alive, much less talk about how I felt now. They wouldn't understand. No one could.

I was vaguely aware that Mrs. Sandel was introducing someone and I looked up again.

"Students," she said, "I would like to present Lieutenant Grady Johnson of the Homicide Division, who is investigating Mrs. Rothlis's death. Please give him your attention."

The man in the dark suit came forward and cleared his throat. I looked into my lap again. I didn't want to see him or hear what he had to say.

"Good morning, everyone," he began. "Mrs. Rothlis's death has been ruled a homicide, and a suspect has been taken into custody."

Near pandemonium broke out in the gymnasium as the students reacted to the news, but I could only sit frozen to the spot, my heart barely beating.

Suddenly arms encircled me and Keeley was whispering, "It can't be Drew. And even if it is, it's a mistake. You know that, too, don't you, Ashlyn?"

I slumped against her, nodding and swiping away tears at the same time.

By now Mrs. Sandel had the crowd under control, and Lieutenant Johnson was speaking again. "Even though we have a suspect, our investigation is not over. We have Mrs. Rothlis's appointment calendar. Detective Walt Granbeck, also of the Homicide Division, will be assisting me in checking with all of you who either saw her or were scheduled to see her yesterday. I'd like to request that any of you who think you may have noticed something out of the ordinary at school yesterday to please come forward. No matter how small or insignificant it may seem, I or Detective Granbeck would like to talk to you. It might be more important than you realize. We'll be in Mrs. Sandel's office all day today. Please stop by to see us."

"Thank you, Lieutenant Johnson," said Mrs. Sandel, returning to the podium. "You may go to your classes now, students. The assembly is dismissed."

As I moved along with the crowd toward the gymnasium exits, a new panic struck me. Drew's name would be on Mrs. Rothlis's appointment book, and even worse, it was probably the last appointment scheduled for the day—the one closest to the time she was murdered.

chapter

7

All morning students whose names were in Mrs. Rothlis's appointment book were called out of class and asked to report to the office. Still, by second period rumors were flying around school that Drew Jansen had been arrested for Mrs. Rothlis's murder. I couldn't stand not knowing for sure, and so I hurried to the pay phone outside the gym as soon as the bell rang to change classes and called his house.

I thought for a moment that no one was home again, but after the eighth ring his grandmother answered.

"Hello, Mrs. Jansen, this is Ashlyn. I was wondering about Drew. I haven't seen him at school this morning, and . . . ." I couldn't finish. How could I ask her if Drew was in jail?

I didn't have to. She told me herself.

"Ashlyn, dear, I have some very bad news. The police have accused Drew of murdering Mrs. Rothlis. They came to the house last night and asked him a lot of questions. Then they came back this morning and told him that he was under arrest and . . . and took him to jail." Her voice quavered. Then she sighed heavily and went on. "I called a lawyer and then posted bond for him a little while ago, right after his arraignment. He's home now. The judge set his trial date for March seventh. That's only six weeks away, but you know of course that he's innocent, don't you?"

"Yes, Mrs. Jansen, I *do* know. Drew told me what really happened. He can explain everything. And besides, why would he want to kill Mrs. Rothlis? She was his *friend*. What kind of motive for murder is that?"

My voice had risen almost an octave while I was talking. I took a deep, calming breath and went on in a slower, quieter tone. "May I speak to him?"

"He's sleeping now, dear. He's totally exhausted from his ordeal, and I hate to wake him. Would you mind calling back after school? I promise to tell him you called as soon as he wakes up."

"Sure. I'll call again when I get home."

I replaced the receiver and leaned forward, resting my forehead against the cool surface of the tall pay phone. I closed my eyes and tried to talk my heart into beating more slowly. Drew Jansen had *not* been arrested for murder. And Mrs. Rothlis *wasn't* dead. Those things happened only in the dark tunnel of nightmares, and any moment I would wake up to the sunshine of an ordinary day.

The yellow crime-scene tape stretched across the door to Mrs. Rothlis's office was a garish reminder of why the police were stationed in Mrs. Sandel's office. I went to my next class racking my brain for some clue to who the real murderer was. Had Mrs. Rothlis found out some horrible secret about a student or another faculty member? And had that person killed her to keep her quiet? It sounded pretty far-fetched. Still, you read about things like that in the newspapers all the time.

Or maybe she interrupted a drug deal. My mind tried to conjure up the picture, but it couldn't. First, anyone who was dealing at Quentin Sargeant wouldn't do it after school in the counselor's office, and that was where her body was found—in her own office.

What about her personal life? I wondered. Admittedly, I didn't know much about it. The rumor mill said she was a widow. What if she wasn't? What if she was divorced and her ex-husband showed up? Maybe he used to like to beat her up—that's why she divorced him—and he beat her up again, only this time he killed her? Or a boyfriend. Maybe she had an abusive boyfriend. A hothead. A total freak-out. Lots of girls had boyfriends like that. Boyfriends who were jealous and liked to use their girlfriends as punching bags. Look at

April McCarthy. She went with that jerk, Devin West, and everybody knew he was like that.

April and Devin. My heart began to pound. April had come in to see Mrs. Rothlis yesterday morning, and she had been crying. Had she talked to the counselor about Devin? And had Devin found out and come after Mrs. Rothlis? It could have happened that way.

I thought about April for the rest of the morning. I wanted to talk to her. I knew she probably wouldn't confide in me, but I wanted to try anyway. I watched for her in the halls between classes, but I didn't see her or Devin West.

On our way to McDonald's at lunchtime, I ran my theories by Keeley. She listened patiently while she drove, looking especially interested when I came to the part about April and Devin and how frightened and upset April had looked.

"The police have probably talked to April by now," she said. "After all, they have Mrs. Rothlis's appointment book."

"Yeah, but . . ." I sputtered. "But April didn't have an appointment. Remember what I told you? She knocked on the door during first period while I was working in Mrs. Rothlis's office. Unless she's come forward on her own, I'm probably the only person besides herself who knows she went to see the counselor."

"Except maybe Devin," Keeley added soberly.

"Right," I replied, nodding. Suddenly I wasn't hungry anymore.

By the time we got back to campus I had made up my mind to tell the police about April. They hadn't called me out of class this morning since working as a student aide meant my name wouldn't be in the book either, and I couldn't believe that April had gone to see them voluntarily.

The bell was ringing as I nervously approached the door to the principal's outer office. I could see the Homicide investigator whom the principal had called Lieutenant Grady Johnson through the glass pane. He was sitting at a small desk in the corner of the office, looking through some papers. I shuddered involuntarily. Had he been the one who had arrested Drew? I stared at him, half afraid to approach him. Still, I had to tell someone about April and Devin. Talking to him would take only a moment.

"What can I do for you?" the officer asked as I entered the office and stopped beside his desk. His voice was pleasant, and he didn't look like an ogre. In fact, his hair was graying and thinning on top, giving him a grandfatherly look.

I took a deep breath and began. "I'm Ashlyn Brennan and I'm . . . I mean, I was Mrs. Rothlis's student aide. I usually worked for her first period."

"Well, Ashlyn, thank you for coming in," Lieutenant Johnson said pleasantly. "Won't you sit down."

I nodded and sank to the edge of the wooden chair beside the desk. Mrs. Rothlis's appointment book lay open on the desk in front of him, and there were several pages of handwritten notes scattered about. A framed picture of the counselor holding Dumpster sat nearby. He pulled a clean sheet of paper out of the desk drawer and printed my name across the top.

Any composure I had suddenly evaporated at the sight of a police officer writing down my name. I knew it was ridiculous, but I couldn't help wishing I had never come to see him.

"Did you work for Mrs. Rothlis yesterday morning?" asked Lieutenant Johnson.

My throat suddenly felt too tight for words to pass through, and I nodded again.

"How did she seem?" he asked. "Normal? Worried? Frightened?"

"Just—just normal," I stammered. "She laughed and talked the way she always did."

"Then nothing unusual happened while you were there?" he prompted me.

I hesitated. This was it. For an instant I was sorry I had come. Poor April had enough trouble without my telling the police that she came to see Mrs. Rothlis. *But what about Drew?* a little voice demanded. *He's innocent, and he's been arrested!*

"There was one thing that happened that I thought you should know about," I said.

Lieutenant Johnson leaned toward me. "Go on," he

said. "And take your time. Just tell me what happened."

I did as he asked, relating how April McCarthy had knocked at Mrs. Rothlis's door and asked to talk to her. Her eyes were red and puffy and she definitely had been crying. Then, when she saw me, she shrank back, finally agreeing to come in when I left the office.

"I don't know what she was so upset about," I said, "except I do know that she fights with her boyfriend a lot, and that there are rumors that he hurts her sometimes."

"Do you mean he's physically violent?" asked the officer.

"I've never personally seen him hit her or anything," I added hastily.

"Ummmm," murmured the officer, nodding and scribbling notes under my name.

I must have sounded like a total gossip, I thought, out to ruin another girl's reputation. I glanced toward the door, wishing I could leave. I was already late for class.

"Is there anything else you'd like to add?" asked the Lieutenant.

"No," I replied.

The officer smiled kindly. "Thank you for coming in. I know this has been difficult for you. If you think of anything else, don't hesitate to come back."

Lieutenant Johnson rose and extended his hand. As

I shook it, I glanced at the picture of Mrs. Rothlis and Dumpster again.

Suddenly my hand stopped in midair. Dumpster! Why hadn't I thought of him before? Poor Dumpster was alone. Of course Mrs. Rothlis hadn't gone home to feed him last night, and even if the police had searched her apartment, they might not have paid any attention to a cat. It was possible that they hadn't even realized he was there. I couldn't let the poor cat starve.

"There is one other thing. I happen to know that Mrs. Rothlis had a cat. This one," I said, pointing to Dumpster in the picture with Mrs. Rothlis. "Have the police been to her apartment yet? Have they taken care of him?"

Lieutenant Johnson looked at the picture and thought a moment. "Yes, we went to her apartment around seven last night, but I don't remember . . ." He stopped, looking amused. "Hey, wait a minute. We did hear something rustling around behind the curtains, but it never came out where we could see it. Actually, we thought it was probably a mouse."

"That was Dumpster—her cat. He likes to play hide and seek," I said, feeling relieved.

"I'm glad you brought Dumpster to our attention," said the Lieutenant. "It would have been a real shame to let the poor thing starve. I guess when I wrap things up here after school, I'd better go get the cat and take him to the Humane Society shelter, since Mrs. Rothlis didn't have any family nearby." He cocked an eyebrow and looked at me. "Unless, of course, you'd like to take him home with you."

I looked at him in surprise. I hadn't thought about that possibility. Mom would have a fit if I brought a cat home, but of course she would be in Tallahassee for the next few days. Besides, I didn't want Dumpster taken to a shelter, humane or not, and I liked the idea of having him with me. He had been so special to Mrs. Rothlis.

"Okay," I said on impulse. "I'll take him."

Lieutenant Johnson nodded. "Great. I'll meet you at the squad car after school, and we'll go get him."

I left the principal's office and headed back to class with my head spinning. I had gone in to try to help Drew by telling the police about another possible suspect, and I had come out with a cat!

chapter 8

When the dismissal bell rang I stopped by Keeley's locker to explain why I wouldn't be riding home with her and then hurried to the front of the school where the police car waited at the curb. It felt strange, climbing into the front seat beside the officer, and even stranger as we joined the line of traffic streaming away from the school. Kids in some of the other cars looked us over suspiciously. I shrank down in my seat, knowing that some of them were probably thinking that since I was Drew's girlfriend and he had been arrested for Mrs. Rothlis's murder, that I was going to be arrested as an accomplice.

He must have noticed how uneasy I was, because as soon as we were out in traffic he looked over at me and said, "Sorry about the black-and-white. I usually drive an unmarked car, but it's in the shop, getting worked on."

As we rode across town, I reminded myself that the real reason I was there was to rescue Dumpster. As uncomfortable as I felt sitting next to Lieutenant Johnson in a police car, it would only take a few moments to get the cat, and then I would go straight home and call Drew.

Officer Johnson turned into the parking lot of Mrs. Rothlis's apartment and pulled into a space near the stairway leading to her door.

"Okay, here we are," he said almost cordially.

I followed him up the stairs and stood aside while he produced a key and opened the door. Then he gestured for me to enter ahead of him.

I thought my heart would break when I stepped into the dimly lit room. It was exactly the way I remembered. The shades were pulled to keep out the afternoon sun just as they had been the day I visited. Had that only been last week? Everything else looked the same, too. The same comfortable clutter was on the overstuffed sofa, and I could see the teakettle sitting on the stove in her tiny kitchen. She couldn't be dead, I thought as tears gathered behind my eyes.

Just then something gray and white zipped past me in the shadows, gently grazing my leg and then disappearing behind the sofa. I jumped involuntarily and smiled.

"Dumpster!" I cried. "Here, kitty, kitty. You must be starved."

When he didn't reappear, I called again.

"Dumpster? Where are you? Please come out. I want to feed you."

Still no Dumpster.

"Maybe if you get out some food, he'll smell it and come out then," suggested the officer.

I shrugged, feeling stupid for not thinking of that myself, and went to the kitchen. Two empty bowls sat on a folded newspaper on the floor beside the counter. I went to the fridge and got out milk, which I poured into one of the bowls. Then I looked around for food.

Suddenly I stopped. "Is it all right if I touch things?" I asked.

Grady Johnson nodded. "We've just about finished here. It's just the crime scene we're still protecting. We'll probably keep it closed off for another twenty-four hours to make sure we haven't missed anything."

I didn't answer. I couldn't bear to think of Mrs. Rothlis's office as a *crime scene,* so I busied myself opening cupboards and looking for cat food. Opening the third door, I heard the clanking of metal. Inside were several small hangers embedded in the wood holding a variety of tagged keys. One of the tags read "Spare apartment key." I glanced around. Lieutenant Johnson's back was to me, so on an impulse I grabbed it and stuffed it into the pocket of my slacks.

In the next cupboard I found cans of cat food. "Here, Dumpster. Don't be shy," I called as I emptied the smelly stuff into the second bowl.

As soon as the fishy aroma hit the air, Dumpster streaked into the room and dived for the bowl, slurping up the food as fast as he could.

I stood there watching Dumpster eat and thought about how Mrs. Rothlis had taken him in off the street. He would probably have starved to death if she hadn't rescued him. And now she was the one who was dead.

"Ready to go, Ashlyn?"

"Yeah, I guess so," I said reluctantly. Dumpster had finished eating, and I gathered him in my arms, listening to him purr as I looked around one last time.

Why? Why? Why? I wanted to shout as I gazed lovingly at the homey apartment and the things in it that were so much a reflection of Mrs. Rothlis's personality. A pair of old sneakers, one with the toe out, sitting on the floor beside the footstool. A heart-shaped candy dish on the coffee table. A stack of magazines on the floor beside the easy chair.

My gaze stopped at a pair of framed pictures on the wall behind the sofa. I hadn't noticed them when I was there before. The larger one was a picture of a baby girl in a silver frame. She had the face of a cherub and a wide grin that showed one tooth protruding through the bottom gum. She was so cute that I had to smile back at her. I stepped closer. Engraved into the silver frame was the baby's name: Heather Rothlis. Puzzled, I squinted at the picture again. Mrs. Rothlis had never mentioned having any children. Was baby Heather her daughter? Just above the baby's picture was a smaller, slender wooden frame, holding a yellowing piece of needlepoint. The background had once been white, and stitched in precise lettering and bordered by faded pastel flowers was a poem:

GOD GIVES EACH ONE OF US
ONE DEAR MOTHER
SO THAT NOBODY NEED FEEL SLIGHTED,
AND ONLY ONE
SO THAT NOBODY NEED FEEL TOO PROUD.

I read the words again, a lump forming in my throat. It was exactly the sort of sentiment Mrs. Rothlis would like.

Dumpster was starting to squirm, so I boosted him higher on my shoulder and headed for the door. Lieutenant Johnson was standing there, one hand on the knob, watching me. I swallowed self-consciously, keeping my eyes down.

"Aren't you going to take the cat food?" he asked kindly. "Save you a trip to the store."

"Oh, sure," I said, trying not to let him see that I was flustered.

I turned to head back to the kitchen when he stuck out a hand holding three cans of cat food.

"I got it for you while you were looking around. You really liked her, didn't you?"

He was looking at me with sympathy, and I felt tears well up in my eyes. I nodded, not caring for the moment that he was a policeman. What was important was that he understood.

"Yeah," I murmured. "I liked her a lot."

As we were leaving Mrs. Rothlis's apartment, the door to the apartment just to the left of hers opened and a middle-aged man stepped out.

"Excuse me, Officer. May I speak to you for a moment?"

I glanced at the man, who had a red bushy beard and a balding head. Hovering near his elbow was a mousy-looking woman.

Lieutenant Johnson stopped and waited for the man to approach him. "What can I do for you?"

"Sir, my name is John Michael and this is my wife, Lucy. We've lived next door to Mrs. Rothlis ever since she moved in, and we were awfully sorry to hear that she was . . . that she died." He shifted from one foot to the other, and I could tell from the uncertainty in his voice that he had something else he wanted to say.

"That's kind of you, Mr. Michael," said the officer. "You didn't notice anything unusual around here in the past few days, did you?"

Mr. Michael looked relieved. "Yes, sir." Then he looked worried again. "It might not be anything, but Mrs. Rothlis didn't have any company to speak of.

Then the night before she was . . . she died, a man came to visit her."

My stomach turned a flip-flop. I hugged Dumpster closer, holding my breath.

Lieutenant Johnson pulled a notepad and pencil out of his pocket and began to write. "Did you get a look at him?"

Lucy nodded. "It was a hot night, and we had our windows open. I just happened to glance out when I heard someone coming up the stairs. I'd say he was about forty years old, real thin, with short, dark hair. He knocked on the door, and when she opened it, she seemed real glad to see him. Invited him right in."

"He didn't stay very long, though," her husband broke in. "Couldn't have been more than a half hour."

"Did you hear any sounds of an argument?" asked the officer.

My heart quickened, but both Mr. and Mrs. Michael shook their heads.

"What about his car? Did you get a look at it?"

Mr. Michael looked sheepish. "Never gave it a thought. I mean, we had no idea . . ."

"Of course you didn't, sir," Lieutenant Johnson said gently. "Thanks for coming forward with the information. I may need to ask you more questions later, if it's okay."

The Michaels looked at each other and then nodded at the officer. "Anytime."

Except for Lieutenant Johnson's asking directions to

my house, we rode home in silence. It was all I could do to keep from shouting at him that he should drop the charges against Drew. There were plenty of other suspects. Devin West for one, and now the mysterious man who had visited Mrs. Rothlis the night before she was murdered. But I kept quiet, afraid I'd say the wrong thing and make it worse for Drew. I also had my hands full with Dumpster, trying to keep him from bolting out of my arms. He obviously didn't care for riding in cars, and I was grateful when we finally pulled up in my driveway. I stuffed the cans of cat food into my pockets, thanked Lieutenant Johnson, and hurried into the house.

Dumpster exploded out of my arms the instant we were inside the door. In one continuous motion he hit the floor and bounced into Mother's favorite white leather chair by the living room window, immediately settling down to wash an invisible spot off a paw.

I groaned, thinking how she would absolutely freak out if she were there to see it and was about to grab the big gray-and-white cat and give him a good talking-to about what was not allowed in this house when Greta appeared from the kitchen.

She was a short, round woman whose long, gray-blond hair was swept up into an elaborate mass of curls that were bobby-pinned tightly to the top of her head. A year and a half ago she had lost her left breast to cancer, but she never stopped humming John Philip Sousa marches while she worked. She never padded the left side of her chest, either. I considered her a very brave woman, but then, I guess you'd have to be brave to work for someone as particular and demanding as my mother. This afternoon her usual smile was gone.

"Was that another police car I just saw in the driveway?" she asked, frowning. Then spotting Dumpster, her eyes got wide and she blurted out, "Where did that thing come from?"

"This is Dumpster," I said, gathering up the cat again and rubbing my chin against the top of his silky head. "He needs a temporary home."

"You know how your mother feels about animals," Greta warned. "Have you checked with her about this?"

I shook my head. "It's just for a couple of days, until I figure out what to do with him," I said. Then I explained where he had come from and why I had brought him home in the first place.

Greta reached out and tickled him under the chin. "Poor little lamb," she said, sounding more like her old self. Then abruptly she straightened and looked at me with a frown.

"Did you say that this cat belonged to that counselor from your school? The one who was murdered?"

I nodded. "Why?"

"Because that's what that other policeman was here about." Greta wrung her hands and looked apprehensively toward the door.

The expression on her face startled me. "What are

you talking about, Greta?" I demanded. "What other policeman?"

"The one who was here just after lunch. He was looking for your mother. He even took the telephone number of the hotel where she's staying in Tallahassee. He said he had to talk to everyone who had an appointment with the counselor yesterday. He called her Mrs. Rothlis. Wasn't that her name? The one who was killed?"

I stared at Greta and then gave a cynical laugh. "*My* mother had an appointment with the school counselor? What would she be doing there, anyway? I'm not having any problems in school."

"I don't know, Ashlyn," Greta said earnestly. "But the policeman said he needed to talk to her because she had an appointment with Mrs. Rothlis right after school."

Dumpster was wiggling in my arms again, so I put him down softly and chuckled.

"Don't worry about it, Greta," I said. "Unless Mrs. Rothlis had suddenly gotten interested in the environment, it has to have been some kind of mistake."

chapter

9

This time Drew answered when I called the Jansen house. At the sound of his voice I forgot all about how calm I had planned to be and blurted out, "Drew, are you okay? Tell me what happened!"

"Hey, calm down. I'm out of jail now, and everything's cool."

"Oh, sure. It *isn't* cool," I insisted. "Not if the police think you killed Mrs. Rothlis. Come on, Drew, tell me what happened."

"Okay. Here goes." The sound in his voice was ominous. "They got here about nine o'clock last night, and the first thing they said was that someone had seen me leaving the school in my truck just before Mrs. Rothlis's body was found. They also said that they had her appointment book and knew that I had made an appointment to see her during last period and wanted to know why."

"What did you tell them?"

I heard him draw in a deep breath. "I screwed up. I lied."

My heart stopped. "What do you mean?"

"I told them that I had gone to see her about information on colleges. I thought it made sense since I'm a senior, and they seemed to buy it. Then they asked why I hadn't kept my appointment. That freaked me. How could they know I didn't show up? I got really flustered. Mumbled something about forgetting. Then I did something really stupid. I asked them how they knew I missed my appointment. They said she made a notation.

"Then they wanted to know why I went back after school. Ashlyn, you can't believe how much that shook me up. I tried to explain. I told them I was sorry for skipping out on my appointment and went back to see if I could still talk to her and that I panicked when I found her body and ran."

"What did they say? Couldn't they understand why you would do a thing like that?"

Drew didn't answer for a moment. "It was about that time that they noticed a bloodstain on the left knee of my jeans. I didn't even know it was there. I must have gotten it when I tried to give her CPR."

"Didn't you tell them that?" I insisted.

"Of course I told them. But they took my jeans anyway. They're going to run them through the lab to see if the blood matches Mrs. Rothlis's blood. Naturally it will. They read me my rights and hauled me off. And when we got to the station, they fingerprinted me. They said they found a fingerprint in the blood on the floor. That will match, too, of course. And that's not even the worst of it."

I took in a long, slow breath and closed my eyes. "Drew, tell me the rest," I whispered.

He was silent again. "I had to take a drug test while I was there."

"So? You're clean."

"I lied to you about the night I spent in Keeley's dock house, Ashlyn. It was nothing big. I just smoked a little grass, and I've been clean ever since. I swear I have. The only trouble is I won't test clean."

I was too stunned to answer for a moment. Drew had given in to Andy, after all. And worse, he had lied to me about it. I tried to ignore the ache in my heart. I would think about that later. Drew was in trouble. A lot worse trouble than I had ever imagined.

"Oh, Drew," I whispered. "What are we going to do?"

"Don't worry," he said, sounding more shaky than confidant. "Gram's been on the phone, and she's already got me a lawyer. He's supposed to be pretty good."

"I know. Your grandmother told me. She said the trial's in six weeks. That isn't very long."

"Don't sweat it," Drew insisted. "This guy's really good. He's got a terrific record of acquittals. He won't let me go to prison."

Prison. It was unthinkable.

"And, Ashlyn," Drew said just above a whisper. "I didn't lie when I said I had nothing to do with Mrs. Rothlis's death. You've got to believe that. I just have to prove it."

"I know. Oh, my gosh! I almost forgot," I sputtered. "The police have some other leads. You're not the only one they're investigating." I went on to tell him about April and Devin and my theory about them, and also about the man Mr. and Mrs. Michael saw at her apartment the night before she was killed. "It's only a matter of time before you're cleared," I assured him.

Drew sighed heavily.

"Hey, don't get down on yourself. It's going to be okay. The police are going to dig until they find the truth. And you know I believe you. I know you wouldn't hurt anyone, much less Mrs. Rothlis. Oh, Drew, I love you so much, and I promise I'll stick by you and help you get out of this awful mess no matter how long it takes."

"I'll tell you the same thing that I told the police," my mother said. "Mrs. Rothlis called me and asked me to come to her office that afternoon to inform me about Drew Jansen's drug habit and to warn me about allowing you to continue your involvement with him."

"What!" Her words hit me like a tidal wave, and I reached for the kitchen counter to steady myself.

"But he doesn't have a real drug habit," I started to say, and then didn't. I would never convince her now because he had made one lousy mistake and failed one lousy drug test. Besides, it suddenly didn't matter what my mother thought, because I had been betrayed. It was impossible, but it was true. How else would she know about Drew's problem? Mrs. Rothlis had *told* her.

I had just gotten home from the funeral and found that Mother had returned from Tallahassee while I was gone. She was sitting in the breakfast room, sipping iced tea and taking long, deep drags on her cigarette. I knew that upstairs in her bedroom were five pieces of perfectly matched luggage, waiting for Greta to unpack them.

"I was going to discuss it with you that night," she went on, her voice softening a little. "but I had a million things to do to get ready for my trip the next morning, and you were so upset about her death when I came to your room later. I decided that it would be best to postpone bringing it up until I got back." She paused for a moment. "You can't imagine how surprised I was when the police telephoned my hotel while I was on business with the governor and said they wanted to talk to me. Naturally I told them that she was very much alive when I left her office around four."

I watched her blow a cloud of smoke into the air and stub out her half-smoked cigarette in an ashtray, immediately lighting another one. I studied her face for signs that she was making up the story, but how could she? There was only one place she could find out about Drew's problems: from Mrs. Rothlis.

"What exactly did she tell you?" I asked, still testing. "About Drew, I mean."

Mother sighed. "That she was looking into some ways to get him help. Talking to some psychiatrists, I think she said. She had a file on him an inch thick, but she wasn't terribly optimistic. She said he'd been addicted since he was a child. I'll bet you didn't know that, did you?"

I winced at the triumph in her voice. "No," I said just above a whisper. I had to lie. I had to buy time to get hold of myself.

"I was right about Drew Jansen all along, of course," she said angrily. Then she sighed and leaned toward me, reaching out to take my hand. "Sweetheart, you have to be so careful about whom you associate with these days. The schools are full of alcoholics, drug addicts. You're too good for people like that. Your father and I have given you so many advantages, such a wonderful future. It would be a tragedy to get mixed up with a boy like Drew Jansen and throw it all away."

I felt myself recoil inside, and I pulled my hand away from hers. She had finally said what I knew she had been thinking all along, that Drew wasn't good enough for me.

I don't know how I managed to leave her presence and make it to my room, but somehow I did. I fell across my bed, sobbing. I didn't care who heard. I couldn't hold it back any longer. I had told Mrs. Rothlis Drew's terrible secret, and she had gone straight to my mother. The counselor had been the one adult I thought I could trust, and look what she had done. She had betrayed me. It was unbelievable. How could she have done a thing like that? And after I had cared about her so much. And thought that she had cared about me.

I rolled over on my back and thought about the funeral. It had been a nightmare. Naturally Drew had stayed away, but Keeley and Greg and I arrived at the funeral home chapel in time for the viewing before the service began. It took all the courage I had to approach the casket. Then it took another moment to look at her face. My eyes shot to her temple, but thankfully makeup covered the spot where the blow had been. Her face looked so alive and yet somehow cold and plastic.

"Are you ready to sit down?" Keeley whispered after a few minutes.

I shook my head. "Go ahead," I whispered back. "I want to stay here a little longer. I'll be there shortly."

Greg looked at me with concern. "Will you be okay?" he asked.

Nodding, I watched him follow Keeley to find three seats together among the rows of folding chairs filling the small chapel. Most were already filled, and I glanced around the room to see teachers and classmates from Quentin Sargeant High School somberly waiting for the service to begin.

When I turned back for one last look at Mrs. Roth-lis, to say good-bye, I was aware that a man and woman were approaching.

"Thank you for coming," the woman began. She was probably in her sixties, and she had short, dark hair streaked with gray and dark circles under her eyes. "We're the Jacobses, her mother and father." She nod-ded toward a gaunt-looking man who stared silently into the coffin.

"Oh," I said. "I'm Ashlyn Brennan. I'm really sorry. She was . . ." I couldn't finish.

Mrs. Jacobs nodded and sniffed into a tissue. Then she looked up bravely again and said, "We're from out-side Atlanta, and—" Her voice broke off suddenly. She was trying so hard to remain composed that she looked as if she might explode any second.

Her husband shook his head in disbelief and mur-mured to no one in particular, "So much tragedy in her life . . . so much tragedy."

"I'm really sorry," I repeated, looking straight at Mr. Jacobs this time. I didn't know what else to say.

He shook his head again and murmured. "First her husband, then her baby, and now this. So much tragedy. So much."

"The baby?" I asked, remembering the picture hanging on the wall of Mrs. Rothlis's apartment.

Mr. Jacobs looked as if he were about to say more when his wife abruptly said, "That's enough, Herbert. All that is over and done. Let poor Judy finally rest in peace."

He nodded and lowered his head in sorrow.

I didn't hear a single word spoken during the service. I sat between Keeley and Greg, clutching each of their hands and telling myself that it wasn't really happening. Then suddenly it was over, and I came home. Home to the news that Mrs. Rothlis had betrayed me.

My exhaustion must have overcome me, causing me to doze, because the next thing I knew something warm and furry was snuggled against me, purring loudly.

"Dumpster?" I whispered. I opened my eyes to see his yellow eyes staring straight into mine. His whiskers twitched when I said his name again, and he snuggled closer.

We lay there comforting each other for a long time. I stroked his silky coat and tried to keep my mind blank. I didn't want to think about any of the things going on around me. The possibilities were too terrible to contemplate. But I couldn't keep the thoughts away.

What was going to happen now? I had lost the one

adult I trusted to help Drew. I had been sold out. Drew had been arrested for a murder he hadn't committed and could spend the rest of his life in jail unless Lieutenant Johnson came through and found the real murderer.

I sat up, cuddling Dumpster under my chin. But what if he didn't? He hadn't acted very interested in April and Devin. What if he didn't even talk to them? And there were lots of other kids at school he should talk to, too. There were tons of troublemakers who got sent to see the counselor over and over again. Sometimes kids had come to see her about problems at home. Violent problems at home. She heard all kinds of terrible secrets, things a lot of people would resent her knowing. And then there was the man who had visited her the night before she died. Lieutenant Johnson had written down everything that the Michaels had told him, but he had also said he *might* talk to them again. That didn't sound like a crack Homicide investigator out to catch a murderer. What if there was so much evidence pointing to Drew that he didn't even try?

chapter
10

After Mrs. Rothlis was killed and Drew was accused of her murder, the mere act of getting up and going to school every day became one of the hardest things I have ever had to do. I was hurt and angry, but in addition to that, I was still in shock. That first morning after the funeral I headed down the hall like a zombie. All I could think about was how I *should* have been going to her office to work as her student aide, just as I had been doing every day since the beginning of the school year. I should have been, but I wasn't. I couldn't. Not ever again.

I shook myself back to reality and looked at the closed door I had just stopped in front of. My heart lurched.

"Oh, no," I whispered. "What's wrong with me?"

The name plate on the front of the door read MRS.

JUDITH ROTHLIS, COUNSELOR. In my stupor I had automatically come here. The yellow crime-scene tape was
gone now, and the door looked just as it had every
morning since I started working for the counselor.

As I backed slowly away, the door opened, and
Mrs. Sandel emerged, looking sad and tired.

"Ashlyn?" said the principal, registering surprise at
seeing me there.

"Hello, Mrs. Sandel," I mumbled, feeling a little
foolish. "I was . . . I . . ."

"Oh, Ashlyn, it's nice to see you. How are you
getting along?" Her face relaxed a little.

"Fine," I said. I smiled at her and tried to act casual.
"I was thinking about something else and I must have
automatically come straight here. I worked for Mrs.
Rothlis first period."

"Yes, I know. It's such a tragedy to lose her," she
said. "Now that the police are finished in her office, I
have the sad task of packing away her personal things so
they can eventually be turned over to her parents."

I nodded, thinking that packing up Mrs. Rothlis's
belongings would be hard, and once they were gone it
would seem as if she had never been there. It would be
just another office. And what if there was one remain-
ing clue among her things? Something the police had
missed? The idea almost blew me away. I couldn't go in
there. Or could I?

"Mrs. Sandel, I'd be glad do it for you," I said

quickly before I could change my mind. "In fact, I usually worked for her first period, so I could start right now."

"Why, Ashlyn, I would really appreciate that," said the principal. "It should only take a couple of hours, so you could probably finish tomorrow."

Mrs. Sandel ushered me into the office, thanked me again, and promised to go straight to one of the custodians and ask him to bring me some boxes. The next thing I knew, I was alone.

My heart was in my throat as I glanced around at the familiar clutter. The stacks of books and magazines and file folders interspersed with smiling-cat plaques, sleeping-cat figurines. Cats, cats, cats everywhere. Memories pressed at me with an almost physical force.

I moved toward her desk, dropping my books into the chair facing it. I stared at the chair. Was that where the murderer had sat? The reports in the newspaper had said that nothing was taken from Mrs. Rothlis's purse and the office had not been ransacked, leading police to speculate that she knew her killer. Had they started out having a friendly conversation and then something went wrong? Had the person suddenly gone berserk? *Had Andy come back?*

The thought startled me. I knew Drew was innocent, and yet I couldn't ignore the fact that he had given in to Andy and then lied to me about it. I prayed that it was only that once. If only he had kept his appointment and had gone to see Mrs. Rothlis earlier. Maybe she had information that would have helped him. Or maybe he had another reason for going to see her so late. Maybe Andy had come back again, and he needed her more than ever. Or . . . My heart stopped. I couldn't let such an awful idea into my mind. I could never doubt Drew and believe that Andy had gained control over him. Never, never.

I hadn't heard Mr. Claxton come into the room. Suddenly his face was in front of mine, and he was saying, "Are you all right, miss?"

"Sure, I'm fine," I said, and grabbed a pair of boxes out of his hands.

"Here's some newspaper, too, for wrapping the fragile stuff," he said. He looked me over critically. "You sure you're okay?"

I nodded and busied myself clearing a spot on the desk for one of the boxes. As soon as he left, I sank into the counselor's chair, burying my head in my hands. How could I possibly have even the smallest suspicion that Drew might be guilty? Of course the murderer had covered his tracks well. He had wanted someone else to look guilty. I had to stop spinning my wheels and start looking for clues.

For the rest of the hour I carefully wrapped and packed away the objects that had been so precious to the counselor, keeping an eye out for anything out of the ordinary. I didn't find anything worthwhile. A few things were out of their regular places. And I didn't see the cat paperweight that usually sat on the corner of her desk, but that could have been moved, too. The police officers had probably picked up everything in the office during their investigation. Naturally they wouldn't remember where everything went.

It was almost time for the bell to ring ending first period when I remembered the file on Drew that my mother said Mrs. Rothlis had shown her. I knew it existed. She had started it when I confided in her about Andy and asked for advice on how to help him. She had never let me see the notes she took on our conversations, but I wanted to see them now. I needed to know why she had felt that it was necessary to betray my confidence and tell my mother about Drew's problem. Had Mrs. Rothlis done some investigating on her own? And had she found out something so awful that she felt she could go only to my mother?

I went through everything on the desk carefully. When I didn't find it the first time, I searched again. It wasn't there. That had to mean that she had filed it away again after Mother left the office. Methodically, I thumbed through each of the *J* files looking for Jansen. It wasn't there. Next I tried *D* for Drew. If she had filed it herself, she might have absently stuck it in the wrong place. Finally, in desperation, I looked under *A* for Andy. Still no file. *That's really strange,* I thought. Had it contained something so terrible that she had to hide it?

As I closed the last file drawer I remembered my

suspicions about April McCarthy, and I pulled open the drawer marked *L–P* and thumbed through the *M*s until I found a file with her name on it. It was a new file, with only one sheet of paper in it, an interview with April dated the day Mrs. Rothlis died. I took April's file to the desk and sat down to read it.

April came to my office first period and asked to talk privately. Red, puffy eyes. Obviously had been crying. April said that her boyfriend, Devin West, was jealous of everyone she talked to, even girlfriends. Restricted her activities. No freedom to spend time with friends. Said she had tried repeatedly to reassure him that she cared for him but to no avail. Lately he had begun hitting her and threatening her with more abuse if she told anyone. Showed me bruises, placed where they wouldn't show. Afraid to talk to parents. Afraid violence would continue to get worse. Advised April to ask Devin to stop in and see me. She protested, saying he would be furious. Told her I would send for him if she was afraid to speak. She said she would talk to him herself and try to convince him to see me. I said the sooner the better. Tell him to come in today.

I collapsed against the chairback, both relieved and frightened by what I had just found out. Devin West was a violent person who abused his girlfriend, and the counselor had known it. He had threatened more violence against April, so it was logical that he could have stormed into the office and blown up at Mrs. Rothlis for interfering. He could have killed her in a fit of rage. The bell rang then, and I slipped the file back into its place, shutting the drawer. I would have to make sure that Lieutenant Johnson knew it was there.

Drew did not return to school, even after the yellow crime-scene tape had been removed and student life had pretty much returned to normal. For the first few days he stayed away on his own because he needed time to pull himself together. Then Mrs. Sandel called Camille Jansen and told her that since her grandson had been charged with the murder of a faculty member, the school board felt it would not be wise for him to return to Quentin Sargeant High until after the trial. She said that his assignments would be sent to him once a week by a student so that he wouldn't lose out on his schoolwork, and naturally I jumped at the chance to be the one who took the assignments to him.

The first batch of assignments was ready on the second and final day that I packed up Mrs. Rothlis's office. I had called the police department and left a message for Lieutenant Johnson about April's file, and I was dying to tell Drew what I had found out.

I rushed home right after school and went straight to the phone. I knew he worked today, and I wanted to catch him before he left the marina.

The telephone rang and rang, and I was just about

to hang up when a familiar voice answered, "Shark River Marina. Jeff speaking."

"Hi, Jeff. It's Ashlyn. Is Drew still there?"

"Yep, he's down in the engine compartment of a thirty-four-foot Bayliner. Want me to call him?"

"No, that's okay. Just tell him not to leave until I get there. I'll be by in *Mellow Time* in half an hour."

"I'll tell him," said Jeff.

"Thanks," I said.

I hung up the phone and changed into a purple-and-teal-striped bikini, throwing an oversized purple tee on over that. Next I grabbed a couple of beach towels and headed for the kitchen, rummaging around in the fridge to see if Greta had left something to make into a picnic supper.

Ten minutes later I backed *Mellow Time* out of its slip and headed up the canal.

chapter
11

There was a light chop on the water, and I watched a lone pelican pass overhead, cocking his head and looking down at me as if asking for a handout.

"I'm not a fisherman, silly," I called up at him.

He hovered off my stern for another few seconds and then wheeled away in search of better prospects.

When I reached the juncture where ours and a dozen or so other small canals flowed into a larger one leading to the open waters of the Gulf of Mexico, I glanced toward the Strachans' dock. The small one-room dock house perched on the end of the dock looked deserted now, but in my mind I could see the soft light that had glowed in the window the night Keeley had called to say that Andy had come back to torment Drew. Nothing had been the same since then.

I gunned the engines once I left the protected water

and sped north along the coastline. I was heading away from the residential areas toward the busier commercial district and Shark River Marina. The light chop of the inland waters had turned into two- to three-foot seas offshore, but it was still a comfortable ride as the boat went up on plane and skipped lightly across the surface. I could hardly wait to see Drew. I knew he would come with me to Sand Dollar Island. We picnicked there so often that it was practically a ritual. I would wait until we got there and the moment was right to tell him my news about April.

Boat traffic was unusually heavy as I turned inland again and followed the red-and-green markers that lined the channel. Pleasure boats of all sizes were coming in from a day on the water, and the commercial fishing boats I met were heading out to sea for the night's catch.

Drew was waiting at the gas dock with a towel draped around his shoulders when I turned *Mellow Time* into the marina. He threw lines to me when I pulled up alongside and cut my engines. I squinted up at him in the late-afternoon sun, feeling the same rush of happiness that always came when we were together. It wasn't just that he was handsome, which he was, with his blue-green eyes and suntanned face. It was his manner. His style. His quiet strength and his calm smile. It was hard to imagine what he was going through.

I secured the boat and hopped onto the dock, standing on tiptoe to give him a quick kiss.

"Hi," I said saucily. "Waiting for a ride, by any chance?"

A grin spread across his face, and he answered in a husky voice, "You bet. Where're we going?"

"I'll tell you in a minute," I replied. "Do you have any change for the soda machine? We were out at home."

Drew nodded and dug into his jeans pocket. A few minutes later we had dumped the cans into the cooler and were casting off. Then he went below and changed into a swimsuit that he kept in the cabin.

It took about twenty minutes out in the Gulf to reach Sand Dollar Island. The low, finger-shaped island was less than a half mile long and only thirty to forty yards wide. Ringed with a beach of sugar-fine sand, the center was covered with tall marsh grass and a few scrubby pines. We could see that it was deserted, which was pretty normal for the middle of the week, although on Saturdays and Sundays boats usually dotted the shoreline. Easing back on the throttle, I ran the boat straight toward the beach, slowly heading in bow first until it grazed the sand, and cut the engines while Drew secured the stern anchor. Then he hopped off and pulled the larger bow anchor onto the beach, burying it in the sand.

Once the boat was secured, we began to unload the

picnic supplies and beach gear. Filling my lungs with the fresh, salty air, I watched a flock of wading birds scatter as Drew carried the cooler and a couple of beach bags up to a level spot in the sand. I followed behind, lugging the towels and a pink-and-green-striped beach umbrella. When we finally got the umbrella set up and a plastic tablecloth spread under it, I began digging around in the cooler.

"This is kind of a strange picnic," I said, pulling out a hunk of Jarlsburg cheese in plastic wrap and a lump of aluminum foil containing cold fried chicken. "I had to bring what was in the fridge. No time to go to the deli." Next I dug out a jar of kosher dill pickles and two containers of chocolate pudding. "Sugar free," I said proudly, pointing to the pudding. "There are crackers and chips in one of the beach bags. Hope you're hungry."

Drew pulled me to my feet and into his arms. "I sure am," he whispered. He kissed me tenderly at first, looking deep into my eyes with such love that my heart almost burst. He kissed me again and again, deeper and harder, growing more and more needful.

I responded totally. Drew was my happiness. He was all I needed, and when I was in his arms, the rest of the world didn't exist.

I wriggled out of his arms and raced for the water, laughing and calling back over my shoulder, "Hey! I think you need a cold shower."

Drew plunged in after me, diving under the water and grabbing me around the knees. I took a deep breath just as he dragged me down beneath the surface for a fast underwater kiss. We came up together, sputtering and laughing, the water bubbling around us.

"Do you always go swimming in your T-shirt? Or did you forget to wear a suit?" he teased.

Glancing down, I realized that I had completely forgotten to take off the shirt before diving into the water. Now it clung to me like dew. "See what you do to me?" I demanded, faking indignation.

Drew rolled his eyes. "Yeaaaah," he said, and dived for me again.

"Oh, Drew, I love you so much," I said as we walked back up onto the beach hand in hand a little while later. "I could never imagine us not being together."

I knew instantly that I'd said the wrong thing. He stopped in the sand and looked down at me, his happy mood evaporated. "Baby, you don't know how much I've missed you and how scared I am right now. The cops told my lawyer that all they need to guarantee a conviction is the murder weapon. God, Ashlyn, do you realize that I could go to prison for something I didn't do?"

His eyes looked frightened, and I closed my own eyes and held him as tightly as I could. The fact that Drew might go to prison was something I had forced myself not to think about. For years I had heard stories about what went on in prisons, but it had seemed somehow unreal. Besides, I had always told myself that it was a shame but it didn't concern me. That nobody I knew would ever have to face it. That those guys probably deserved what happened to them, anyway. Now I swallowed hard and tried to recapture that feeling of unreality—for Drew's sake.

"It'll be okay," I said. "You're not going to prison. Wait until I tell you what I found in Mrs. Rothlis's office. A file on April McCarthy." I told him about the interview notes and how the counselor had told her to send Devin West to her so that she could talk to him. "April was terrified of him. Can't you just see Devin storming into Mrs. Rothlis's office and telling her to stay out of his life and when she wouldn't, going berserk and picking up something and hitting her?" I was breathless from excitement when I finished, but Drew's solemn expression hadn't changed.

Drew sighed. "They've got a witness who saw me leaving the school just a couple of minutes before the custodian found the body. They've got my fingerprints on her desk and phone and a bloody fingerprint on the floor, not to mention her blood on the knee of my jeans. And they're going to try to convince the jury that since I failed the drug test, I'm heavy into drugs. Do you seriously think that with that kind of evidence, they're going to worry very much about a girl who's afraid of her boyfriend?"

I bit my lower lip, refusing to admit that I saw his point. I would talk to Lieutenant Johnson myself and make sure he talked to April.

"All you have to do is say the word 'drugs' to a lot of people," Drew went on, "and they imagine somebody freaked-out enough to commit murder. And according to my attorney, that's how the prosecution is going to try to portray me."

"How can they do that?" I asked.

"They'll build a scenario something like this: I was really going to go to see Mrs. Rothlis about my drug problem. I chickened out. Left school and got high and then came back. When Mrs. Rothlis saw that I was high, she said something that made me mad. We argued. I got hot and then picked up something and hit her."

"But it's your word against theirs about why you went to see her," I insisted.

Drew shook his head sadly. "Don't forget what your mother told the police—that Mrs. Rothlis called her into the office to warn her not to let you keep on seeing me because I was on drugs. You know they'll ask her to testify. If only I hadn't given in to Andy that night. Then I would have tested clean and they wouldn't have such a good case."

Sighing, I tried another tack.

"Didn't you say that your grandmother hired one of the best criminal attorneys in the country? He'll know how to prove your innocence."

Drew shook his head and shrugged helplessly, slogging through the sand toward the beach umbrella where our picnic lay, uneaten. "It would sure help if they'd find the murder weapon. Maybe the murderer still has it, or if he doesn't have it, it's at least covered with his fingerprints. I don't know. I keep thinking that if they could just hurry up and find it, I'd be off the hook. Then it wouldn't matter that Andy got me that night. They would know I didn't do it."

I hurried to catch up with him. "But why, Drew? Why *did* Andy get you that night, of all nights?"

Drew slapped his thighs in frustration. "I don't know. I just couldn't handle him that night." He stopped in front of me, looking directly into my eyes. "That's why I went to Keeley's dock house, to fight it out with him. But it's like you said. I can't do it by myself. I need help. And now the person who could help me is dead. Oh, God, Ashlyn, I'm so sorry. Sorry that I didn't keep that appointment. Sorry that I went back later. Sorry that I found her that way." He dropped to his knees in the sand and buried his face in his hands. "You'll never know how sorry I am."

He began to cry softly. I didn't know what to say for a moment. I knelt beside him, thinking about how special he was. In spite of being the great-grandson of the founder of the community and living in a mansion, he was as comfortable as old sneakers. He drove a pickup truck instead of one of the preppy BMWs or

Mercedes that crowded the high school parking lot, and he worked after school as a boat mechanic. How down-to-earth could you get? He was real. He was kind and gentle and loving. And he was trying hard to deal with Andy. Drew Jansen definitely was not a murderer. I couldn't let anything stop me from helping him prove it.

I pulled his face toward mine and kissed away the tears streaming down his face. "It's going to be okay," I said, hearing the conviction in my own voice. "I promise you, it's going to be okay."

chapter
12

Three things happened the next day that complicated things. First, I talked to Lieutenant Johnson.

I went straight to the pay phone when I got to school that morning and called the police station, asking to speak to him. When I told him who I was, he sounded glad to hear from me and asked about Dumpster. We made small talk for a few minutes, and then I got to the point of my call.

"I was wondering if you got my message about the file on April McCarthy that I found when I was packing up Mrs. Rothlis's office?"

There was a pause. "Yes, Ashlyn, we did check out the file and appreciate your detective work. We spoke with April McCarthy and she assured us that she was going to speak to Devin West about going to see Mrs. Rothlis but changed her mind. She also said that Mrs.

Rothlis had apparently misinterpreted what she said and had thought things were worse between herself and Devin than they really were. I'm sorry, Ashlyn, but with that kind of statement from April, we don't feel it's necessary to proceed any further."

She's lying! I wanted to shout. *She's trying to protect Devin, and she'll say anything.* I fought to calm myself. Getting emotional wouldn't help a thing.

"Well, what about the man who visited Mrs. Rothlis's apartment the night before she died?" I asked. "Have you found him yet?"

"No, Ashlyn," the officer said in a tone of voice that told me he was trying very hard to be patient. "We haven't located anyone else who saw him. We haven't given up, but these things do take time, you know. Thanks for calling. We always appreciate it when private citizens come forth with information."

I knew I was being dismissed so I said good-bye and hung up. The police weren't checking April's story any further, and they weren't looking for the man who came to Mrs. Rothlis's apartment. They were so convinced that Drew was guilty that they weren't even bothering to look for someone else. Well, I wasn't going to give up. I was going to keep looking and digging and asking questions until I found the real murderer.

The second thing that almost ruined my day was that Mom found out about Dumpster.

Every morning before I left for school I made sure

his litter box was clean and that he had water and food in his dishes. Since he slept most of the time when I was around, I supposed that was what he did while I was at school, too. So I would close the door to my room, leaving him inside, and feel pretty secure.

I had started feeding him dry cat food instead of canned because he ate only half a can at a time. The rest needed to be refrigerated, and I was afraid Mom would find it. Maybe that ticked him off. I don't know. But what I do know is that Mom met me at the door that afternoon, her eyes blazing.

"What do you mean by hiding a *cat* in your room?" she demanded, puffing on her cigarette and blowing smoke like an enraged dragon. I couldn't remember when I had seen her so angry.

Cringing on the inside, I tried to put on my best face. "So you've met Dumpster, huh? He belonged to Mrs. Rothlis. I'm only keeping him for a few days until I can find a good home for him."

"Dumpster," she spat out contemptuously. "Well, at least he's appropriately named. You know I'm allergic to cats. I want that mangy thing out of this house immediately, good home or no good home. Is that clear?"

"But, Mom, he isn't mangy, and he's no trouble," I pleaded. "He just stays in my room and sleeps. I promise you'll never know he's here, and I'll find a home for him as fast as I can."

"Ashlyn, I already *know* he's here. He frightened

me half to death a little while ago. I heard crashing sounds coming from your room, and when I went in to investigate, that *thing* had gone berserk and turned over half your potted plants and was clinging to the top of your curtains."

The look on Mom's face told me I had better not laugh, even though the image of Dumpster swinging through my plants like Tarzan and landing high atop the jungle-print curtains almost forced me to do just that.

"You know how I hate cats," she warned through clenched teeth. "Now just get him out of here."

There was no use arguing. I would have to find someone to take him. But first I would have to do some damage assessment in my room. Still amazed at my mother's outburst, I hurried to the door, opened it a crack, and looked in. My heart sank. Mom was right. Dumpster definitely had gone berserk. I swung the door open the rest of the way and went in. My room looked like a war zone. Half a dozen plants lay on their sides, dirt dumped onto the floor. Leaves and palm fronds were scattered everywhere, and even the real Tarzan, my stuffed gorilla, was in a corner on his head.

Dumpster was nowhere to be seen. He had evidently tired of his perch on the curtains. Or maybe my mother had frightened him into hiding. The last option seemed the most probable.

"Here, Dumpster. Here, kitty, kitty," I called, and scanned the dark corners of the room.

I was sure he was there somewhere, peering out at me from his hiding place and trying to assess how much trouble he was in. I wanted to reassure him, so I picked up his food bowl and shook a little dry food into it from the bag on my desk.

"Here, Dumpster," I coaxed again, holding out the bowl like a peace offering. "Suppertime. Come on, kitty, kitty."

He wasn't having any of it. Not supper. Not me. So I finally put his bowl down and started straightening up the mess. That was when the third major disaster of the day occurred.

The phone rang.

"Ashlyn, have you seen tonight's paper?" Keeley demanded as soon as I answered.

"No," I said. "I just got home."

"Well, you'd better read it, but just be sure you're sitting down."

"Why? Keeley, what's wrong? It isn't about Drew, is it?"

There was a pause. "Yes, and about his parents. The police found them, living a skid-row existence on the streets of south Miami. Naturally, the authorities are making a big deal out of it."

I exhaled a big puff of air. "You're kidding."

"Don't I wish. Do you want me to read it to you?"

"Absolutely," I said.

"Okay. Here goes.

" 'It was revealed today that police have located Quentin and Darcy Jansen, parents of Andrew Jansen, the eighteen-year-old man who has been charged in the murder of high school counselor Judith Rothlis. The Jansens, both attorneys, moved their local law practice to the Miami area almost eight years ago. Shortly after that Andrew Jansen, then ten years old, came to live with his grandmother, Camille Jansen. Mrs. Jansen is the widow of Peter Jansen, prominent local banker, and the daughter of Quentin Sargeant, who developed this area of southwest Florida from swampland into what it is today.

" 'Area residents who were friends of Quentin and Darcy Jansen reportedly tried unsuccessfully to contact the Jansens after their move to Miami, leading to widespread speculation about their possible disappearance, although no formal investigation was ever launched by the Jansen family.

" 'Late today, authorities found the Jansens living in a makeshift shelter constructed of cardboard boxes in a drug-infested area of south Miami known for its large homeless population.

" 'Neither Camille Jansen nor her grandson could be reached for comment.' "

"Wow," I whispered, shaking my head. "Drew said that since he failed the drug test at the jail that night, the prosecution will try to portray him as a freaked-out drug addict capable of anything, including murder. Now that they've found his druggie parents, he'll look even worse. And what if the police find out about what they did to him when he was little?"

"You mean Andy?" asked Keeley. "How could they find that out?"

"I don't know, unless they dig into his rehab records and there's something about Andy there. All I do know is, things are really building up against him and building up fast. I'm scared."

Keeley didn't answer for a minute, and I knew she was trying to think of something reassuring to say.

"You know, sometimes I think this whole mess is my fault," I said, feeling a rush of guilt. "If I hadn't pressured Drew into going to see Mrs. Rothlis in the first place, he wouldn't have gone to her office that afternoon and found her body, and he wouldn't be charged with murder right now."

"Come on, Ashlyn. Give yourself a break. You know you can't blame yourself. You were doing what you thought was right and what you thought was best for Drew. You couldn't possibly have known that somebody was going to murder Mrs. Rothlis. Or that he was going to skip his appointment and come back later, after she was dead."

"But there's more to it, Keeley," I said quietly. "There are some things I haven't told you yet."

I took a deep breath and began relaying my mother's story about how Mrs. Rothlis had called her and set up the appointment to warn Mom that Drew was back on drugs and that I shouldn't be seeing him.

"What!" Keeley shrieked. "She said *that* to your mother, knowing how much you're trying to help Drew?"

"I know it sounds incredible, but Mom can't be lying about that, and believe me I've figured every angle. How else would she know that Drew went to Mrs. Rothlis for help? He couldn't have told her, and I certainly wouldn't, and nobody else knew. Can you believe that? She sold us out!"

I was almost in tears when I finished. Every time I remembered Mrs. Rothlis's betrayal, the anguish started all over again.

"Oh, Keeley, I just thought of something else," I said, feeling a sudden chill. "Mom said Mrs. Rothlis told her that he had been addicted as a child. She also said Mrs. Rothlis had a file on him an inch thick. Do you think she showed Mom what was in that file? If she did, Mom could already know about Andy."

"Don't you think she would have told you if she knew a thing like that?" reasoned Keeley. "You'd just better hope that the police don't find Drew's file and read it themselves."

"Oh, my gosh," I said. "When I was packing up Mrs. Rothlis's personal things in her office, I looked all over for Drew's file. I couldn't find it anywhere. Maybe the police already have it."

chapter
13

As the days went by my frustration grew. I had been looking for April McCarthy ever since my conversation with Lieutenant Johnson, but she hadn't been in school. I didn't believe that she was sick. I had been working in Mrs. Rothlis's office when she came in that morning wanting to talk, and she knew that Drew Jansen was my boyfriend. It wouldn't have been too hard for her to put two and two together after the police talked to her and figure out that I had been the one who had told them about the file. It was obvious that she was afraid to face me.

Finally one morning I spotted her walking across the courtyard before school. I told Keeley that I'd see her later and caught up with April. She turned absolutely pale when I approached.

"April, I need to talk to you," I said, stopping directly in front of her. "I think you know what it's about."

"Me?" she said, trying to look surprised. "No, I have no idea what you'd want to talk to me about."

"You lied to the police, didn't you?" I demanded. "You *did* tell Devin to go see Mrs. Rothlis that day. And he went, and you're scared that he may have lost his temper and killed her, aren't you?"

April looked at me in horror. "No, no, it didn't happen that way at all. I told the police the truth. Well, at least mostly it was the truth. I didn't change my mind about talking to Devin. I chickened out. I was afraid of what he'd do to me for going to see her in the first place. You don't know him. He can be . . ."

Her voice trailed off, and her eyes widened as she gazed over my left shoulder. "Oh, hi, Dev," she said with a nervous laugh. "I've been looking all over for you."

I glanced around to see Devin West swaggering toward us. He swept reddish-blond hair out of his eyes with his fingers and looked me up and down as if I were a piece of garbage. Then he grabbed April roughly by the arm and led her away.

"What were you talking to her for?" he demanded. "Didn't I tell you to meet me in the parking lot?"

"Ouch, Devin. You're hurting my arm."

I watched them go, feeling sudden pity for April. She was definitely under Devin's thumb. She had to lie for him to save her own skin. But how could I find out for sure if he went to see Mrs. Rothlis? There was no way that I could confront Devin myself.

In the meantime, Mom stayed on my case about Dumpster. I tried hard to find him a home, but after a couple of days I was starting to get desperate. Keeley had a dog, and Greg's mom had allergies. The circumstances were all wrong to ask Drew. I inquired around at school, too. When they found out it was Mrs. Rothlis's cat, a few kids acted interested, but nothing came of it.

The threat of the Humane Society loomed over me. I knew what that meant. If they couldn't find a home for him in a week or ten days, euthanasia. I couldn't blame them. They were overrun with homeless cats. But I couldn't stand the thought of Dumpster being put to sleep. I kept thinking how ironic it would be for him to end up the same way his mistress had.

I was feeling pretty desolate when an idea hit me like a thunderbolt. There was someone who might sincerely want Mrs. Rothlis's cat. Someone who had been close to her and would like to have Dumpster as a remembrance. Her parents.

I called Keeley right away.

"What do you think about my contacting Mrs. Rothlis's parents about taking Dumpster?" I asked.

"I think it's a great idea," said Keeley. "But do you know their names and how to get hold of them?"

I thought a minute. "I met them at the funeral. They said their last name was Jacobs. I'm not sure where they live, though. They were pretty vague about that. Somewhere near Atlanta, I think they said."

"Maybe you could call the police station and ask for Lieutenant Johnson," she offered. "The police probably were the ones who contacted them after she was murdered."

"Ummm," I murmured, thinking that I didn't really want to talk to Grady Johnson right now. "I have a better idea," I said quickly. "I'll call the funeral home. Surely they'll know. Mr. and Mrs. Jacobs must have taken care of all the arrangements since they shipped her body back to the Atlanta area for burial after the funeral."

As soon as I got off the phone with Keeley, I called the funeral home. They not only had the name and address of Mrs. Rothlis's parents, they had a phone number as well. I thanked them and then sat at my desk for a long time, staring at the phone number, wanting to find Dumpster a good home, but dreading to talk to Mrs. Rothlis's parents again. How were they handling all this? After all, she had been their little girl. It must be terrible to lose your child, I thought sadly. Maybe they would still be too broken up with grief to talk to me. Or think that I was intruding.

I heard a soft purr and glanced down to see Dumpster sitting on the floor beside my chair. He looked up at me with soft yellow eyes and raised a paw as if he were asking to be picked up. I tried to swallow the lump that was forming in my throat as I lifted him gently into my lap.

"Oh, Dumpster, I don't want to give you away," I said, snuggling him close and scratching his favorite spot behind his ears. "I wish I could keep you forever and ever," I whispered into his fur.

But the memory of my mother's fury brought me back to my senses. I had to find him a good home, and find it soon.

Mrs. Jacobs answered the phone and seemed startled when I told her my name.

"Why, Miss Brennan . . . I'm so glad . . . I mean, I should have . . ." she mumbled.

I was sure she had me mixed up with someone else so I explained that I had been Mrs. Rothlis's student aide and that I had met her and Mr. Jacobs at the funeral.

"Yes, dear, I remember clearly," she said. "And I really do apologize for not getting in touch with you before now. You see, reading Judy's will was a very difficult and emotional experience for us, and we've just simply put off taking care of her bequests."

Now it was my turn to be startled. "Her bequests?" I murmured.

"That's right," said Mrs. Jacobs. "I thought that was why you called. I assumed that Judy had told you that she was leaving you the small needlepoint plaque that hung on her living room wall. She made it herself, many years ago. Apparently you admired it because she only added it to her will a few weeks ago."

"Oh," I mumbled, and stared at the phone in stunned silence. I remembered seeing the plaque when I went to the apartment to get Dumpster.

> GOD GIVES EACH ONE OF US
>
> ONE DEAR MOTHER
>
> SO THAT NOBODY NEED FEEL SLIGHTED,
>
> AND ONLY ONE
>
> SO THAT NOBODY NEED FEEL TOO PROUD.

Why on earth had she left it to me in her will? Was there some kind of message in that poem? I wondered. Had she disapproved of my feelings for Drew all along and was using the poem to tell me to listen to my mother? Was that why she had felt justified to betray me to Mom?

"Miss Brennan? Are you still there?"

"Oh, yes," I stammered. "Actually, I didn't know about the plaque. I mean, I was calling about something else."

"Certainly, dear. I just assumed . . ." Her voice trailed off.

I bit my lip, trying to think of what to say next. Suddenly calling bereaved parents to ask if they would take their dead daughter's cat seemed out of place. Dumpster stretched a paw up toward my face as if to remind me of his importance.

"It's about Dumpster," I began gently.

"Dumpster?"

"Her cat."

"Oh, yes," said Mrs. Jacobs. "I remember him now. A big gray-and-white cat, isn't he?"

"That's Dumpster," I said, stroking his back. "The reason I'm calling is that I've been keeping Dumpster at my house since . . . well, you know." I swallowed hard. "Anyway, my mother doesn't care for cats and says I have to find him another home. Since he was your daughter's cat, I thought you might like to have him."

"Well, I don't know," Mrs. Jacobs responded slowly. "We'll have to think about it. You see, we haven't had any pets in the house since Judy grew up and left home. It would be quite an adjustment."

"Oh, Dumpster's a wonderful cat," I said eagerly. "He's quiet and clean and he's very affectionate."

There was a slight pause, and then Mrs. Jacobs said, "I'll tell you what, dear, Mr. Jacobs and I will be coming back on Monday to clean out Judy's apartment. We'll be there several days, and since we'll be seeing you anyway to give you the plaque, we'll give you an answer regarding the cat then. Is that all right?"

"Sure," I said. "That would be fine."

As soon as we hung up, I snuggled him close again, wondering what would happen to poor Dumpster if they said no.

The next day was Sunday, and I awoke to gray clouds and the threat of rain. A rare cool snap had dropped the temperature into the fifties, and I slipped into a comfortable pair of blue sweats and my old sneakers before brushing my hair and going down to breakfast.

The kitchen is normally quiet on Sunday mornings since Greta has weekends off and Mom rarely makes an appearance before noon. My usual routine is to take a bowl of fresh fruit and the Sunday paper out onto the lanai where I can listen to the birds sing and watch the water sparkle in the canal while I catch up on the latest goings-on in the world.

This Sunday morning was different. Mom was in the breakfast room. She was wrapped in a gray cashmere bathrobe, taking deep drags on her cigarette and sipping coffee while she read the front page of the paper. She was also wearing reading glasses, which she whipped off the instant she noticed me standing there.

"Good morning, Ashlyn," she said pleasantly.

I held my breath, worried that she would ask about Dumpster, but she didn't, so I murmured good morning and began sorting through the fruit in the porcelain bowl by the sink. I wrinkled my nose. Most of it was bruised and soft.

"Why don't you try some of this new cereal," she suggested. "It's really pretty good."

I looked at her in surprise. Somehow I had never imagined Mom as a big cereal eater, although I had to admit that we seldom had breakfast together. The bowl with a milky puddle in the bottom sitting beside her coffee cup must have been hers.

I shrugged. "Sure. Why not?" I picked up the box and read the contents. Grains, fiber, nuts, and raisins. It sounded okay so I poured myself a generous portion, added milk, and settled down with the comics. As soon as she finished with the front section, I looked it over quickly to see if there was any mention of the murder investigation, eager for the police to unearth a clue that pointed to someone besides Drew. There was nothing.

Mom and I sat there in silence, sharing the Sunday paper without sharing a word, or a smile, or a look. In fact, I didn't even notice when she left the breakfast room. Finally all that was left of the paper was the classified ads, so I put my bowl and spoon in the dishwasher and strolled out onto the lanai.

There was a brisk wind rolling dark clouds west toward the Gulf. Storm clouds, maybe, I thought, squinting into the breeze. I had half planned to take *Mellow Time* out today, maybe heading to Sand Dollar Island where I could sit on the beach in solitude and try to figure out how to help Drew. *Not if there's going to be a storm,* I reminded myself.

Sighing, I sauntered back to my room and tried to call Keeley, but no one was home. I glanced at my bed, feeling suddenly sleepy.

"Maybe this would be a good day just to snuggle up with Dumpster and sleep," I said half aloud. The idea was appealing. I hadn't slept well since Mrs. Rothlis was murdered, and each day I felt more and more exhausted. A whole day of doing nothing sounded wonderful.

The moment I stretched out, I felt something furry land on the bed near my feet. I smiled. "Come on, Dumpster. We'll spend the day together."

Meowing loudly, the gray-and-white cat sauntered up the bed, rubbing against my body as he came and stopping at my head to stare down at me.

"I wasn't kidding. Honest." I turned on my side, curling up to make a hollow spot. Dumpster rolled into a ball beside my stomach and proceeded to lick a front paw.

"There's something I'd better tell you," I said sadly. "Tomorrow Mr. and Mrs. Jacobs are coming to empty Mrs. Rothlis's apartment, and they may be taking you home with them."

Dumpster continued to lick his paw as if he hadn't heard a word I had said.

"I really don't want them to take you," I went on, "but I'm not sure what Mom would do if you stayed here. And they seem like nice people, and . . ."

The words caught in my throat, and I had the sudden vision of climbing the stairs to Mrs. Rothlis's apartment the next day and handing over Dumpster, saying good-bye to him for the very last time. I closed my eyes and remembered another day, the day I had gone to that apartment with Mrs. Rothlis. I had loved the coziness of the living room. I had felt at home there, as if I belonged. For an instant I had felt that same way the afternoon Grady Johnson took me there to get Dumpster. I replayed the scene in my mind, calling for Dumpster, and his being too shy or too frightened to come out. Searching for cat food in the cupboards. And then something else. *The key.*

In the days since I had brought Dumpster home, I had forgotten all about taking the spare apartment key from its hook inside the cabinet. I had done it on impulse. I had had no plans for sneaking back in. But now, as I thought about it, the temptation grew stronger and stronger. Today would be my last opportunity. Tomorrow her parents would be here. And in a few days the apartment would be empty, stripped of everything that had been hers. This would be my only chance to look for something that could identify the mysterious man who had gone to see her the night before she died. Since the police weren't going to try to find him, I had to.

I wasn't sleepy anymore as I rolled off the bed and brushed the wrinkles out of my clothes. I would go there right now, before I could lose my nerve. I fished around in my desk drawer, where I had put the key when I undressed that night. When I found it, I headed through the silent house for the garage. I scooted past the imposing black Cadillac, Mom's red BMW convertible, and climbed into Dad's Jeep, stopping just long enough to take a deep, calming breath before starting the engine and backing out of the garage.

It was beginning to rain as I drove across town, and the same sense of tiredness that I had felt earlier caught up with me again, and I swayed ever so slightly in time with the sweep of the windshield wipers. I slowed the Jeep a little bit and began having second thoughts. What right did I have to go snooping among Mrs. Rothlis's personal things? Besides, the police had probably gone through everything anyway.

But what if they had missed something? A threatening letter. A call on her answering machine. Anything.

I parked in the parking lot of the apartment complex and looked around. It was far from full, with only a few cars sitting here and there.

The tiredness was coming in waves now, so that I almost had to drag myself out of the Jeep. *It's just my mind playing tricks on me,* I assured myself. *Just fear, trying to persuade me not to do this.*

The rain was a steady downpour as I slowly climbed the stairs and stopped in front of Mrs. Rothlis's door. I glanced at the windows of the Michaels' apartment next door, but it was dark. Then before I could chicken out, I unlocked her door and went inside.

It was dark and stuffy inside the apartment, and I groped along the wall until I found the light switch. Even in the light there was a depressing gloom hanging in the air. I glanced around at the plants that had been so green and lush when I was here before. No one had watered them since she died, and they drooped sadly.

I tiptoed into the living room, feeling like a thief. What if someone caught me here? How could I ever explain? I had to hurry, but I didn't know where to begin. The bedroom was to my left. I'd start there.

I began opening drawers in the bureau. Bras and panties were in the first one. I started to reach into the drawer to see if anything was hidden in the back and withdrew my hand immediately. I couldn't do a thing like that. It was too personal. It would be an invasion. It didn't matter that she was dead. Gingerly I opened a few other drawers, but they were all filled with personal items, too. Slips, pajamas, sweatshirts.

A jewelry box sat on top of the bureau, but there was nothing unusual or even of value in it. Just the usual assortment of costume jewelry, earrings, a pair of ancient ticket stubs to an Eagles concert. The usual stuff.

I was wasting my time in the bedroom. *In fact,* I thought as I hurried back to the living room, *I'm wasting my time in this apartment. She didn't have any secrets hidden here. It was her home, and I don't belong here.*

I started toward the door and then stopped in front

of the plaque that would be mine in a couple of days. Taking it down, I looked closely at the needlepoint stitches. They were too neat to have been done by a child. And yet I remembered Mrs. Jacobs had said that she had made it a long time ago. Sighing, I read the words again, trying to understand why she had wanted me to have it.

I shrugged and started to hang it up again, but as I slid it down the wall, expecting the wire to catch on the nail, it didn't. Turning the plaque over, I saw that the wire had come loose from one side of the frame.

Sighing with exasperation, I took it to the kitchen and put it facedown on the counter. It wouldn't be hard to fix. I'd just have to thread the wire back through the small eyelet on the side of the frame, pull it through, and then twist it so that it would hold. As I pushed the wire into the eyelet I noticed that the paper backing had come loose along the bottom edge of the frame and a slip of folded paper had begun to work its way out.

That's funny, I thought. Using my fingernails like pincers, I drew the paper the rest of the way out and unfolded it. The words DEATH CERTIFICATE were printed across the top of the form.

I gasped and stared at the name of the deceased:
Ashlyn Marie Brennan.

chapter
14

I don't know how long I stood there in the gloom of
Judy Rothlis's kitchen, staring at my own death certificate and whispering, "It can't be! I'm not dead!"

At first, I couldn't see anything but my name—
Ashlyn Marie Brennan. But as I gradually regained
some composure, I read on. The date of birth was
mine: March 9, 1977. But the date of death was August
17, 1977. That would have been when I was five
months old. I skimmed down the page, looking for
something that would prove it was all a mistake. Father's name: Douglas R. Brennan—that was right.
Mother's name: Cynthia Hoover Brennan—that was
right, too!

What's going on here? I wanted to cry. I stuffed a fist
in my mouth to keep it from escaping. *This* has *to be a
joke! Some kind of hoax! It just has to!*

I stepped back from the counter and took a couple of deep breaths. *Don't lose your cool,* I warned myself. *There must be an explanation for this.* I picked up the death certificate and ran a finger over the official seal embossed into the page. It couldn't be a fake. Not with the seal.

Shaking my head, I began reading again. This Ashlyn Marie Brennan had died in a hospital in Atlanta, Georgia, of natural causes described as dehydration brought on by influenza and high fever.

The words blurred, and I felt tears making wet trails down my cheeks. I looked around the room as if someone would be there to give me an answer. "Somebody made a mistake. I didn't die. I got well. Just look at me, if you don't believe it!"

I don't know how much later it was when I hung the plaque back on the wall and left the apartment, locking the door behind me. I had kept the death certificate, tucking it into the waistband of my sweats. I wanted to go home, take a shower, maybe sleep awhile, before I tried to figure out what it meant. It obviously wasn't my death certificate, but whose was it? And why had Mrs. Rothlis had it? Giving me the needlepoint must have been her way of making sure I saw it. But why didn't she show it to me herself and give me some sort of explanation?

Darkness had fallen, and the rain had stopped, but it had left behind luminous puddles dotting the streets. I felt exhausted. My eyelids were heavy, and I wondered if I had the strength to drive home as I started the Jeep and headed back across town.

Somehow I made it. Mom's red BMW was gone from the garage when I pulled inside. I was glad. I wasn't ready to talk to anyone right now.

No, what I needed was Drew. I needed to feel his arms around me and hear him tell me that he loved me. Then maybe I could begin to sort things out.

Backing the Jeep out of the garage again, I headed for the Jansen estate. Mom would never know. She was probably at the club, hobnobbing with her elite friends.

It took less than five minutes to reach 2 Pirates Bight Lane, and I pulled up under the porte cochere and turned off the engine, drinking in the night air made more fragrant by the rain and listening to the waves washing against the beach. For the first time since I had entered Judy Rothlis's apartment hours earlier, my pounding headache began to subside. Coming to see Drew had definitely been the right thing to do.

I had the same feeling of awe I always had when I pulled into the driveway of Camille Jansen's grand beach house. It had twenty-four rooms and a four-car garage and had been built by Quentin Sargeant at the turn of the century along a gorgeous stretch of beach. It was cream-color stucco with a red-tile roof. My favorite part of the house was an etched-glass elevator sitting just inside the curve of the grand spiral staircase, which had been put in to accommodate Quentin Sargeant in his later years.

Camille Jansen answered the door. She was a small, trim woman with soft white hair and eyes that normally twinkled. Tonight they were filled with worry, and her face looked drawn.

"Oh, Ashlyn, I'm so glad to see you," she said, pulling me inside. "Things have taken another turn for the worse and I don't know what to do." She glanced apprehensively toward the circular staircase that led upstairs to the bedrooms. "You'd better go to Drew. He's in his room. Maybe he'll listen to you."

Just then I heard a door open, and Drew appeared at the top of the stairs, looking down at us from the railing. Was he unsteady on his feet? Or was I imagining it?

"I thought I heard that old Jeep of yours in the driveway," he called out, slurring his words. Come on up."

He said something else, but the sound of his voice was lost in a low rumbling of distant thunder. I shuddered and hurried up the stairs. Something was terribly wrong.

"Drew, what is it? What's happened?"

He grabbed me roughly by the arm and steered me into the bedroom, slamming the door. "I'm dead meat —that's what."

"What are you talking about?" I whispered.

Drew's eyes glinted with anger, and I could see that his pupils were dilated and his face was flushed. "Drew, you're high!"

He gave me a lopsided grin. "Sure. Why not? They're gonna nail me for something I didn't do. So I might as well get high while I can, because when they throw me in jail I won't have to worry about Andy grabbing me *aaaa-nnneeemore!*"

I sank to the edge of his bed, staring up at him. I was too frightened to speak. I had never seen him like this before, and I had no idea what he might do. But there was one thing I was certain of. Drew had lied to me about using drugs when he spent the night in Keeley's boat house, and he was high right now. He had probably been lying about keeping Andy at bay all along.

"Why are you doing this?" I murmured. "Why are you letting Andy take over?"

He didn't answer.

"Why?" I demanded.

Drew shrugged. "I don't even know why you came here. To look at a condemned man? Is that it?"

"Drew, don't say that!" I stood up, reaching out for him, but he backed away, raising his chin as if to dare me to come closer.

"Did Gram tell you that the police were just here?"

"No," I murmured.

He stomped back and forth across the floor, darting

looks at me with cold eyes. "They said they had a warrant to search for the murder weapon. "So they came up here—two of them—and they started going through everything in the room."

"But you couldn't have the murder weapon," I insisted. "You didn't kill her."

His eyes blazed, and his fist crashed into the wall. *"Of course I didn't!* But do you think they believe that? Do you think they *care?*"

I sat on the edge of the bed, cringing. I had never seen Drew so violent.

Then his voice turned soft and sneering. "But they came anyway. And they treated me like dirt while they tried to find something else to pin on me. But they didn't find *this,* did they?" His voice sounded triumphant.

I blinked at him in uncertainty and then realized he was referring to the stash of drugs he'd taken to get high.

My heart was pounding, and I had to fight to keep my voice steady. "Drew, you can't give up. That's what you're doing, you know? You're giving up!"

I ran out of his room and down the stairs, not even stopping to say anything to his grandmother. I had to get out of there. My whole world was crashing down around me.

chapter
15

I drove home in a downpour, too numb to think. When I reached my room I went straight to the marble Jacuzzi tub in the corner of the bathroom and turned the faucets on full blast, dribbling a little bubble bath into the water. I could hardly wait to sink into the tub and let the jets of warm water soothe away the tension from the scene I'd just had with Drew. But as I peeled off my sweatsuit the death certificate fluttered to the floor. I had completely forgotten to show it to him.

It was no wonder, I told myself as the warm water swirled around me. My mind was reeling. Drew had given in to Andy not once, but twice, and if he had done that, had it happened other times, too? Was he trying to hide a drug problem that was much bigger than I had ever suspected?

My bath water had turned cool, and I shivered. *I*

still have the death certificate to deal with, I thought as I listened to the water gurgle down the drain. I wrapped a warm bath towel around me and stepped out of the tub. It had to be a fake, and there was only one person who might be able clear up the mystery of why it even existed to begin with. My mother.

I threw on a pair of shorts and a top and went to see if she had come home yet. I had the death certificate in my pocket. When I didn't find her on the first floor, I checked the garage. Her red BMW was in its place, dripping puddles on the concrete floor. She was here somewhere.

I hurried up the stairs. I could see a thin line of light coming from under her bedroom door.

"Mom? Can I come in?" I called as I tapped on the door.

"What do you want?" I flinched at the testiness in her voice.

"There's something I need to show you," I answered her. "It's pretty weird. I think you'll want to see it."

"Well, just a minute."

When she finally let me into the room I sniffed a couple of times. There was a funny odor in the air. It reminded me of a hospital. I sniffed again, but now all I could detect was Mom's expensive perfume.

"Ashlyn, stop gazing off into space and show me this weird thing you're all worked up about. I told you I'm busy."

"Oh, sure," I said, reaching into my pocket and handing her the folded paper.

She was still dressed for dinner, wearing a black sequined evening gown, which set her in sharp contrast to the room, which was decorated in all white, like the rest of the house, and accented in gold.

I watch her unfold the sheet and look down at the page inside. She froze for an instant, and then without looking up, she said, "My God, Ashlyn! Where did you get a thing like this?"

I wasn't prepared for the question, although I should have been. I certainly couldn't tell her that I had stolen a key to Mrs. Rothlis's apartment and had gone back to rummage through her things. Besides, as far as I was concerned where I found it was not the issue right now.

"It has to be a joke," I said. "But it's so awful. Who would do a thing like that?"

"I asked you a question. Where did you get this?"

"I—I found it," I stuttered.

She looked at me sharply. "*Where* did you find it?"

My mind raced. "At school. When I was in the counselor's office packing up her personal things. Mrs. Sandel asked me to do it since I had been Mrs. Rothlis's student aide," I said breathlessly.

Mom was still looking at me, standing as still as a statue, barely breathing.

"Mom, look at it! It says I *died*," I insisted, reaching for the paper.

She came out of her trance, backing away and pulling it just out of my reach. "I don't know where it came from, Ashlyn," she said, her voice softening a little. "You did the right thing bringing it to me. All I can say is that it is a cruel hoax, and I have no idea where it came from or why your school counselor would have it. I'll destroy it, of course, and I don't want you to make yourself miserable by dwelling on it. Put it completely out of your mind."

I should have felt better, but I didn't. Something about that awful piece of paper still bothered me. There had to be an explanation, and I wanted to know what it was.

"Mom, please don't destroy it," I begged. "May I see it again?"

Mother shook her head. "No, I don't think that would be wise. It's upset you enough already."

She folded the paper once and then again, and while I watched in amazement, she began tearing it into pieces the size of confetti and dropping them into a large ceramic ashtray sitting on a gold-leaf bedside table beside the assortment of prescription bottles holding tranquilizers and sleeping pills, which she claimed she only took when my father traveled.

"Mom! What are you doing?"

I wanted to scoop up the pieces of paper and run back to my room, but to my horror, before I could move she had picked up a cigarette lighter and set the tiny scraps on fire. The flames flared, dying quickly and leaving only a pile of gray flakes in the bottom of the ashtray.

"There, that takes care of that," she said soothingly.

"I can't believe you did that," I insisted. "Now we'll never know . . ."

She gave me a benign look and lit a cigarette. "Ashlyn, trust me. After all, I'm your *mother*."

I don't know how long I sat on my bed, snuggling Dumpster in my arms and watching the gray, rain-streaked sky darken into blackness. My mind was filled with unanswerable questions. Why had my mother set fire to a death certificate with her own daughter's name on it without first trying to find out where it had come from? Why did Mrs. Rothlis have it in the first place, and why was it hidden in a piece of needlework that she had willed to me?

I must have dozed, because a knock at my bedroom door startled me awake. The room was pitch black, and I blinked and glanced at the clock on my bedside table. The crimson readout said 9:35.

"Who is it?" I called.

Without answering, my mother opened the door and marched in. "You didn't come down for dinner so I brought up some chowder and crackers," she said. Stooping slightly, she set a tray on the table beside the clock and then whirled around and left without another word, closing the door behind her.

I clicked on the lamp and stared at the bowl of Manhattan clam chowder. It smelled delicious, and the rich red broth and spicy aroma made my mouth water.

In my lap, Dumpster was sniffing the air and swishing his tail. He meowed softly and inched toward the chowder.

The smell of the chowder was getting to me, too. I hadn't eaten anything since the bowl of cereal I'd had while I read the Sunday paper on the lanai that morning. I went at it eagerly, and it wasn't until I had finished the entire bowl that I realized I hadn't kept out a piece of clam for Dumpster.

"Sorry, old buddy," I said, stroking his head. "I'll go out to the fridge later and sneak you a little milk."

I never made it to the refrigerator. My exhaustion apparently caught up with me, and I sank into a deep, paralyzing sleep. Once a sharp sound like the honking of a horn reached me, and I swam upward toward light like a diver reaching for the surface of the water, but the darkness pulled me back again. Another time, in the middle of a dream, I heard the ringing of a telephone, but when I picked up the phone in my dream, no one was there.

Finally my eyes slowly opened. My tongue tasted

like cardboard, and my arms and legs felt as if they were weighted with rocks. Dumpster was sitting on my pillow, looking down at me and gently patting my face with his paw.

"Okay, I'm awake," I assured him, propping myself on one elbow. "You'll get your breakfast."

I glanced around at the sunlight slanting into the room, making shadows at odd angles for morning.

"What time is it anyway?" Naturally Dumpster didn't answer.

Rolling onto my side, I frowned at my bedside clock. It couldn't be three forty-nine. It was light outside.

Slowly it dawned on me that it must be late afternoon instead of morning. I had slept through the night and on through the whole day. I had missed school. Why hadn't Mom come in to wake me? Or Greta?

I pushed my feet off the side of the bed, trying to shake off the stupor that hung over me. "Wow," I whispered. "I must have been more tired than I realized."

I vaguely remembered that there was something I was supposed to do today. Something important. But what? I dragged myself to the bathroom and splashed cold water on my face. I looked terrible. Then I cupped my hands and filled them with cold water, drinking it down and trying to wash the dry, cardboard taste out of my mouth.

Suddenly I remembered with a start why today was important. Judy Rothlis's parents were coming to town.

16

I was still wearing the shorts and top that I had thrown on when I went to show Mother the death certificate the night before. They were wrinkled from being slept in for so many hours, so I changed into fresh clothes: white stirrup pants and red-and-white-striped sweater. Back at the bathroom mirror, I frowned at the sweaty and tangled mess of dark brown hair hanging to my shoulders, but I didn't have time to wash it. I gave it a quick brushing and applied a little lipstick and blush.

That will have to do, I told myself. I couldn't waste any more time getting to Mrs. Rothlis's apartment to see if the Jacobses were there.

"Meow."

Dumpster sat at my feet, looking up at me. I picked him up and held him close.

"I didn't forget you," I whispered. "I filled your food and water bowls while I was dressing."

He reached out a paw and patted my face again. His plaintive eyes sent a rush of sadness through me. I had the overwhelming feeling that he was telling me he did not want to go to Atlanta to live with the Jacobses. He wanted to stay here with me.

"But I have to go see them, and it's not just about you," I explained. Then I set him on the floor again and rushed out the door.

The house was strangely quiet as I hurried toward the garage. It wasn't quite four o'clock yet. Greta should still be here, even if Mom wasn't.

Maybe Greta's sick today, I thought. That would explain why she hadn't awakened me for school.

As I had suspected, Mom's BMW was gone from the garage. I supposed she was playing golf at the club or out to a late lunch with some of her friends.

I drew in a deep breath as I climbed into the Jeep and put the key into the ignition. The dull headache that had started when I got up was throbbing in my temples now. I really didn't feel like driving across town and talking to Mrs. Rothlis's parents. Surely they would still be in town tomorrow. No, I thought. I couldn't take a chance on missing them.

As soon as I turned into the parking lot at the counselor's apartment complex, I spotted a late-model gray sedan with a peach-and-white Georgia license plate parked near the building. They were here.

I took my time climbing the steps to the apartment, going over possible opening lines in my mind. As usual, nothing sounded right. I would just have to wing it.

The door opened as soon as I knocked. Mrs. Rothlis's father stood there, looking haggard and wiping his forehead with a handkerchief. He glanced at me and registered only vague recognition.

"Hello, Mr. Jacobs. I'm Ashlyn Brennan. I hope I'm not disturbing you."

"Oh, no, dear. Come on in," called Mrs. Jacobs from behind him. She hurried to the door and opened it wider, ushering me in. Large half-filled cardboard boxes sat around on the floor, and the room seemed suddenly bare and devoid of Mrs. Rothlis's personality.

Although Mrs. Jacobs was smiling, her face looked older than it had at the funeral and the silver streaks in her short dark seemed hair more prominent. Even the dark circles around her eyes were deeper, giving her a slightly owlish look. Her eyes glistened with unshed tears as she took my hand and led me across the threshold.

"It's all right," she assured me. "Herbert and I are delighted that you stopped by. We had planned to call, but we weren't sure what time you got home from school."

Mr. Jacobs did not attempt to conceal the pain he

felt. He nodded his head sadly and blew his nose into his handkerchief, looking around at the packing boxes as if he had lost his place and couldn't remember which one he had been working in.

"Can I get you something to drink?" asked Mrs. Jacobs. "I'm sure Judy kept soft drinks in the refrigerator."

"Oh, no. I can't stay long," I said quickly. Then I bit my lower lip, dreading the question I knew I had to ask. "I was wondering if you had made a decision about Dumpster yet? You know, Mrs. Rothlis's cat."

Mrs. Jacobs sighed deeply. "Oh, I don't know," she said slowly. "As I mentioned on the phone, it would be a big adjustment."

I swallowed hard. "I'd keep him if I could," I said in a small voice. I reminded myself that Mom had been raging about Dumpster again and gave him one final reprieve only when I told her that the counselor's parents were considering taking him. "I honestly would," I said with new determination. "It's just that my mother doesn't like cats. Actually, she's allergic to them, and she said that Dumpster will have to go to the animal shelter if I can't find him a home. You know what that means."

"Myrna, maybe we should take him home after all," spoke up Mr. Jacobs. "You know how Judy loved him, and it would be a shame . . ." His voice trailed off, and I knew he was thinking about Dumpster's fate if he were sent to the shelter.

"Well, I guess we could try it," conceded Mrs. Jacobs. "Why don't you bring him by tomorrow. We should be just about finished packing by then and we'll have time to begin getting acquainted with him."

All I could do was nod. Only one more night to snuggle up with Dumpster and listen to him purr. It was going to be like saying good-bye to a dear, dear friend.

I must have moved toward the door without realizing it because Mrs. Jacobs put a hand on my arm and said, "Before you go, I want to be sure to give you this."

She held out the needlepoint plaque. "Here, Judy wanted you to have it," she urged.

I looked down at the neatly stitched poem in the small dark frame, but in my mind I saw instead the death certificate in the name of Ashlyn Marie Brennan.

"Do—do you know why she wanted me to have this?" I stammered. "I mean, I've only visited here once, and I don't remember even noticing it."

Mrs. Jacobs smiled kindly. "Well, I imagine it's connected to the daughter she lost a long time ago." She reached into one of the boxes and drew out an object wrapped in paper. Unwrapping it, she turned the silver-framed baby picture that had hung next to the needlepoint so that I could see it.

"This is Heather, her little girl. There's probably something about you—your manner, your personality—that struck a chord in her. Maybe she hoped that her little girl would have been just like you."

"I don't understand," I said, looking into the smiling face of the dark-haired baby in the picture.

"It was a long time ago," she said sadly.

Mr. Jacobs put down the candy dish he was wrapping in packing paper and said, "You might as well tell her. There's no use keeping it a secret now that Judy's gone."

Mrs. Jacobs's cheeks colored slightly and she looked uncertain for a moment. Sighing, she said, "I suppose you're right. It's just that Judy had so much tragedy in her life. It's so sad to bring it all up again."

"I liked her a lot," I offered. "In fact, I used to talk to her about things I couldn't talk to anyone else about. She was special."

Mrs. Jacobs nodded. "Come over and sit down on the sofa, and I'll tell you the story. Then you'll understand why she stitched that particular poem."

When we were seated on the sofa and her husband had sunk into a nearby chair, she began to speak. "There was a time when our Judy was the happiest girl in the world. She had married her college sweetheart, Carl Rothlis, and had a brand-new baby girl. Then tragedy struck. In July, Carl skidded on a rain-slick highway on his way to work, landing in the path of a eighteen-wheeler. He died instantly, leaving Judy and Heather alone. They were a young couple and didn't have much insurance, so Judy had to go to work to take care of her baby and herself. With her new teaching degree, she got a job at the local elementary school."

Mrs. Jacobs paused, looking down into her lap. "If only I could have taken care of Heather for her. I would have loved to have a baby around the house again, but I had just had spinal surgery, and even after I was back on my feet, I couldn't lift little Heather."

Mrs. Jacobs paused a second time, sniffling back tears.

"Now, Myrna. Don't go blaming yourself again," her husband said softly.

Mrs. Jacobs nodded bravely. "I know. It's just that . . . Well, anyway, Judy put an ad in the local paper for a baby-sitter for Heather, but nobody applied. It ran for two or three weeks, and she was beginning to get desperate. School was going to be starting in just a few days, and she had to find someone to take care of Heather. So she put an ad in the Atlanta paper, hoping someone would be willing to drive out to the suburbs to take the job.

"Finally, the day before school started a young woman called. She said her name was Sally Grant and she had just moved to Atlanta and needed the job badly. She promised to send for references from the town she had moved from, so with that promise, Judy went ahead and hired her. She didn't think she had any choice, and she thought the young woman seemed very nice."

Mrs. Jacobs glanced fearfully at her husband, reaching out for his hand.

"It's okay, Myrna," he said, taking her hand and kneeling beside her. "Go ahead and finish the story."

"Well, Sally Grant arrived on the first morning of school, and Judy left for her new job. "But then—" Mrs. Jacobs broke off, ragged sobs stifling her words for a moment. Finally she regained herself and went on. "But then when Judy got home from school, Sally Grant and Heather were gone, and Judy never saw her little girl again."

My mouth dropped open, but I was too stunned to speak.

"The police never found a trace of Sally Grant or Heather. Judy never gave up looking for her daughter and believing that she was alive. She found the poem in an old book, and liked it so much that she stitched it to remind herself that she was Heather's only true mother, and also to give to Heather someday when she came home."

I looked from one of Mrs. Rothlis's grief-stricken parents to the other and then down at the poem in my hands. Suddenly the words took on new meaning. They were more than just a lovely tribute. There was something almost sacred about them, like a prayer.

GOD GIVES EACH ONE OF US
ONE DEAR MOTHER
SO THAT NOBODY NEED FEEL SLIGHTED,
AND ONLY ONE
SO THAT NOBODY NEED FEEL TOO PROUD.

"So you see, you must have been very special to Judy for her to want you to have this," Mr. Jacobs said gently.

I was too overcome with emotion to do anything but nod. It was true. There *had* been a special bond between us. I had felt it from the very beginning.

So why had she betrayed me to my mother? And why was a death certificate with my name on it hidden behind these beautiful words?

chapter
17

I heard the phone ringing in my room as soon as I entered the house. Mom's car was still missing from the garage, and my footsteps sounded like tap-dancing as I hurried across the white tile floor.

When I got to my room I dived for the phone, belly flopping across my bed and grabbing it on at least the eighth ring. "Hello."

"I was just about to give up. Where have you been?" Keeley's voice was heavy with exasperation. "This is the umpteenth time I've called today."

I winced and glanced fearfully at the phone, feeling as if Keeley could see my face and know that I was about to lie. I couldn't tell her everything. Not yet. I hadn't yet figured out what it meant myself.

"I wasn't feeling well, so Mom let me sleep in," I said. "I did go out a little while ago, though. I went over to Mrs. Rothlis's apartment to talk to her parents about taking Dumpster."

"Oh, yeah," said Keeley. "I had forgotten all about that. What did they say?"

"They're going to do it. I have to take him over tomorrow after school. I'm really going to miss him, you know."

"I know," Keeley said sympathetically. "Would you like for me to come along for moral support?"

Surprised, I asked, "Would you really do that?"

"Sure," she said, "I'll even drive."

Just then a familiar *beep-beep* sounded on the line. "Uh-oh, I've got another call," I said. "Can you hold on?"

"Okay."

I pushed the call-waiting button on the phone and said hello.

"Ashlyn, I'm at the club and I won't be home until late," my mother said crisply. "Greta's off for a few days, so I thawed some spaghetti sauce for you. You'll have to get by on your own this evening."

"That's okay," I said.

She hung up before I could say more. She hadn't even asked if I felt okay, as if sleeping the day away were perfectly natural.

I punched the call-waiting button again. "Keeley, are you still there?"

"Yeah, so what else's new?"

I almost couldn't hear her question over the rumbling of my stomach, reminding me that I hadn't eaten since the bowl of chowder last night.

"Spaghetti!" I said, laughing. "Mom's not home, but she thawed spaghetti sauce for me. How about joining me in a feast?"

Keeley groaned. "Don't tempt me. I got on the scales this morning and found those three pounds I thought I lost last month. I'm living on rabbit food until I get them off again."

"Suit yourself," I said. "Guess I'll see you in the morning then. And, Keeley, thanks for saying you'll go with me to deliver Dumpster to the Jacobses tomorrow."

After we hung up, I boiled spaghetti and heated the sauce, devouring every last bite. When I finally pushed away from the table I was stuffed. I put my dishes in the dishwasher, cleaned up the kitchen, and went back to my room. I felt drowsy but I reminded myself that I needed to sort out all the things that had happened in the past two days. Drew's giving in to Andy. His lies. The death certificate with *my* name on it. And the Jacobses' story of the kidnapping of Mrs. Rothlis's baby by the mysterious Sally Grant. I had the uncomfortable feeling that it was all interconnected, but I wasn't sure how, and when I stretched out across my bed I was too full and too sleepy to care anymore. The bed was so comfortable and my eyelids so heavy that I dropped off to sleep instantly. I didn't even know when Dumpster jumped onto the bed and curled up beside me.

The next day went by entirely too fast, and before I knew it, it was time to take Dumpster to the Jacobses. Keeley had raised the top on her convertible just in case he tried to jump out, and I climbed into the front seat beside her, holding on to him securely.

He clung to my shoulder with his front paws as if he knew we were about to say good-bye, and I nuzzled his fur, wishing there were some other alternative.

But Dumpster must have known he was home the instant Mr. Jacobs opened the door, because he jumped out of my arms and began zipping around the room. I hadn't counted on that, and I couldn't help feeling a little bit hurt. I introduced Keeley to Mr. and Mrs. Jacobs, watching out of the corner of my eye as Dumpster made himself right at home, batting around a balled-up piece of packing paper and exploring a couple of the half-filled boxes before settling down in Mrs. Rothlis's reading chair for a nap.

While I was explaining to Mrs. Jacobs about Dumpster's feeding schedule, her husband disappeared into the bedroom, reemerging a moment later carrying a large scrapbook with a dark red cover.

"This was among Judy's things," he said. "She kept it in case . . ." He paused, obviously choked up, and cleared his throat. "Well, in case Heather came home someday. Since you heard the story, I thought you might want to look through it."

"Gosh," I said in astonishment. "Are you sure you want me to do that? I mean, it's so personal."

"Of course we do, dear," Mrs. Jacobs replied. "As I said yesterday, Judy must have felt very close to you to leave you the needlepoint poem in her will."

As I took the scrapbook from Mr. Jacobs I could feel Keeley's eyes boring holes into the side of my face. I knew she was dying to know what was going on, so I told her as briefly as I could about Mrs. Rothlis's baby daughter and the kidnapping. The only thing I left out was finding the death certificate with my name on it in the frame behind the needlepoint. I was planning to tell her about that, too, but I wanted to do it in private.

I sat down on the sofa with Mrs. Jacobs on one side of me and Keeley on the other. Mr. Jacobs hovered nearby. The scrapbook was in my lap, and I took a deep breath and opened it.

The first page looked like a leaf out of a baby book. There were a couple of pictures of baby Heather, hamming for the camera with a single tooth sticking up from her bottom gum and dark ringlets of hair lying softly around her face.

"She was a doll," I said.

"This is Carl just before the accident," said Mr.

Jacobs. He was pointing to a picture of a handsome young man who was holding Heather in his arms. Next to him stood Mrs. Rothlis looking incredibly young.

Keeley must have noticed that, too, because she piped up, "Wow, Mrs. Rothlis sure was pretty."

We all chuckled, but when I turned the page, the laughter stopped. A yellowing newspaper headline was taped to the top of the page.

BABY GIRL KIDNAPPED FROM ATLANTA SUBURB

Below that were several articles giving accounts of the kidnapping. They were the same as the story Mrs. Jacobs had told me yesterday. On the next page was a picture of Heather with a cutline under it that read: HAVE YOU SEEN THIS CHILD?

I turned the pages slowly, reading only the headlines of the newspaper articles. REWARD OFFERED FOR MISSING BABY. NO LEADS IN ROTHLIS KIDNAPPING. DISTRAUGHT MOTHER MAKES TV APPEAL TO KIDNAPPER.

Gradually the newspaper accounts got shorter and the headlines smaller as time passed and Heather Rothlis's kidnapping was no longer news. I felt a heaviness in my heart as I flipped through the blank pages at the back of the scrapbook. Now Mrs. Rothlis would never have the chance to fill in those pages, even if Heather was found.

Mrs. Jacobs sighed sadly as I closed the book and handed it to her. "Finding Heather and the woman who kidnapped her was an obsession with Judy," she said. "For months she looked for Sally Grant in every crowd, in the supermarket, the mall, in traffic. A few times she thought she had spotted the woman, but of course, she hadn't."

"Judy tracked down leads that the police didn't think were credible," said her husband. "In fact, she made such a nuisance of herself that they asked her to stay away and let them do their job. She slowed down some in later years, but she never totally gave up. Every once in a while she'd see a face in a crowd or a picture in a newspaper that would remind her of Sally Grant and she'd be off and running again. A few times she even hired a private detective. You'd think that after more than sixteen years, she could let it rest."

"More than sixteen years," I whispered, staring at Mr. Jacobs. "May I see the scrapbook again?"

Mrs. Jacobs slid the book across my lap, and I opened it to the first accounts of the kidnapping. I checked the date of the crime. August 24, 1977.

I stared at the date as puzzle pieces began falling in place in my mind. Heather and I were just about the same age, five months old in August of 1977. My father had just come home from Morocco in August 1977, and my mother brought me home to Florida from Chicago. She could have passed through Atlanta on the drive home.

I heard a small cry escape from my lips as I remembered the date on Ashlyn Marie Brennan's death certificate. August 17, 1977—seven days before Heather Rothlis was kidnapped.

chapter 18

Somehow I made an excuse to the Jacobses for having
to leave in such a hurry and half dragged Keeley out of
the apartment, down the stairs, and into her car.

"What's the matter?" she demanded as she plopped
down behind the wheel. "Have you gone berserk?"

"Listen to me!" I began in a breathless voice. "This
is incredible! You aren't going to believe it, but I know
it's true." I gripped her hand and looked deep into her
eyes as I whispered, "I think Judy Rothlis was my
mother."

The instant I said the words, I realized how ridiculous they sounded.

Keeley was staring back at me. "What did you say?"

"You don't know the whole story," I said. With my
heart pounding I told her about sneaking into Mrs.
Rothlis's apartment to look for clues to the murder and

finding the death certificate inside the frame of the needlepoint poem she had left me in her will.

"It was not just my name that was on it, but my parents' names were, too, and that baby died in Atlanta. I knew it was too much to be a coincidence, but until I heard about Mrs. Rothlis's baby being kidnapped just one week after . . . after that Ashlyn Brennan died, I thought it was just some kind of joke."

"I still think it's some kind of joke," said Keeley. "Ashlyn, you can't possibly believe your mother kidnapped a baby and that you're it!"

"I know," I said after a pause. "I guess it is pretty farfetched—I died on the way to Florida so my mother posed as a baby-sitter named Sally Grant and snatched a kid to replace me."

"Right," said Keeley. "Besides, why would she lie about her baby dying? Why wouldn't she just tell your dad the truth, instead of stealing a baby and pretending it's hers?"

"I know it sounds crazy," I said. I tried to agree with the things Keeley was saying, but I just couldn't, except for the part about my mom lying to my dad. I couldn't think of a single reason why she would do that. "You should have seen the look on Mom's face when I showed her the death certificate. And then she tore it into little pieces and set fire to it in an ashtray. Keeley, I have to find out more about the Ashlyn Brennan who died."

Keeley still looked skeptical. "*If* there was an Ashlyn Brennan who died. Okay. Okay. What do you have in mind?"

"Well, I was just thinking, if I told Mom I was spending the weekend with you, and you told your parents you were spending the weekend with me, we could drive up to Atlanta."

"What?" Keeley cried. "What good would that do?"

"Well, we could check the newspaper files. If a baby really did die on August 17, 1977, there would have to be a death notice."

Keeley took a deep breath and let it out in an exasperated burst. "Can't you just call? That's an awfully long drive."

"I want to see it for myself," I said solemnly. "Besides . . . if there's a grave, I want to see that, too."

We talked about it for a while longer, and Keeley finally agreed. We both knew that Mom wouldn't check up on me if I said I was sleeping over at Keeley's. And Keeley's parents trusted her, so they wouldn't check up on her, either.

We decided to leave school at noon on Friday and try to drive as far as Valdosta, Georgia, which was just over the state line from Florida, that first night. We'd get up early the next morning and be in Atlanta before noon. That would give us all of Saturday afternoon to dig around for information. Then we would start out at the crack of dawn on Sunday and try to make it all the way home. It was going to be a long haul, but it would be worth it. In the meantime, since it was only Tuesday, I had the rest of the week to get through.

When Keeley dropped me off a little while later, I let myself in the front door and headed for my room. I could hear my mother talking on the phone in the kitchen. My hand was on my knob when it hit me that Dumpster wouldn't be waiting for me on the other side of the door. I had given him to the Jacobses, and then in all the emotional upheaval of discovering that the date Mrs. Rothlis's baby girl disappeared and the date on the death certificate were just a week apart, I hadn't even said good-bye to him.

"At least Mom will be happy that he's gone," I muttered angrily.

I could hear her voice again, punctuated now and then by a falsetto laugh. *How fake can you get,* I thought.

Turning, I moved slowly toward the kitchen and stopped just inside the family room. It was late afternoon, and the kitchen was ablaze with lights, but no lights had yet been turned on in the rest of the house. I could see her, but she probably couldn't see me standing in the twilight shadows. She was sitting at the kitchen table, still talking on the phone. Papers were scattered in front of her, and the country club directory lay open beside the phone. She was chairman of the club's spring dinner-dance, and I could tell from her

side of the conversation that she was recruiting com-
mittee members.

I studied her angular face. Her ice-blue eyes. Her
perfectly coiffed hair. Her ultra-stylish clothes. She
looked the same as she always had, and yet I realized
that I really didn't know her at all. She had never let
down her guard, and in all the seventeen years she'd
been my mother, I had never once glimpsed the person
behind the mask she wore. A chill ran through me.
Would she have been capable of stealing someone else's
child?

I made my way silently back to my room. Dusk had
turned to total darkness now, but I didn't turn on a
light. I went instead to the sliders, opening them and
stepping out into the cool evening air. A cloud cover
kept the moon hidden, so I flipped on the underwater
light in the pool, watching it bathe the lanai a soft hazy
blue.

I sank down on a lounge chair. *Who am I?* I wondered. *Am I Ashlyn Brennan? Or Heather . . . Heather
Rothlis?* What would happen to my life if I found out
that my suspicions were true? Then I would have to
face the fact that the woman I had called Mother all my
life might be a murderer. It seemed incredible. And yet,
if she had stolen the counselor's baby daughter and had
been tracked down after all these years, she would have
had a motive for murder.

The sudden ring of my telephone made me sit up

with a yelp. I took a deep breath and let it ring a second time before I made a move to get up and answer it.

"Don't let it be Keeley chickening out," I prayed out loud.

It wasn't. It was Drew.

"Hi," he said in a sheepish voice. "It's about time I called and apologized for my behavior the other night. It was stupid."

I wanted to shout at him that it was worse than stupid, but I didn't. "Don't worry. I know you're under a lot of pressure right now."

"Thanks, baby," he said. "What's going on with you? Is everything okay?"

Feeling suddenly panicky, I sucked in my breath and looked up at the ceiling. *No, everything's not okay!* I thought. *I may have been kidnapped as a baby, and the woman I think is my mother may be a murderer.*

But instead, I wrapped the telephone cord around my finger and said nervously, "Things are going okay. I finally found a home for Dumpster. Mrs. Rothlis's parents are taking him back to Atlanta with them."

"That's good news and bad news," said Drew. "I know how much you love him."

"Yeah," I murmured. I could feel tears of regret shimmering in my eyes.

There was a long silence between us, and then he said, "Ashlyn, I need to see you. It's only two weeks until the trial, and I'm getting awfully antsy. I've been spending time with my lawyer every day. He's trying to prep me for the questions I'll get on the stand. It's really scary."

"I don't suppose they've found the murder weapon yet," I said.

"No," said Drew. "I've given up on that."

I sighed in exasperation. "If only we knew what it was. Did they say if they were looking for something specific when they searched your room that night?"

Drew thought a moment. "Not really. Only that it was heavy and blunt. Sort of rounded, I think one of them said. I guess it left an indentation."

I forced myself not to form a picture in my mind and tried to think clearly. "The police said it probably wasn't premeditated. They said it was a crime of passion. That's why presenting you as a druggie will help convince a jury that you could have done it, right?"

"Right, but what does that have to do with the murder weapon?"

"Well, the way I see it, if the murderer wasn't planning on killing her when he went to her office, he probably didn't bring the murder weapon with him."

"Okay, I follow you so far, but I still don't see where you're going," said Drew.

"Then he must have picked up something in her office to hit her with. Maybe something on her desk."

"And?"

"Drew, there was one thing I couldn't find when I

packed away her personal things in her office. The cat paperweight! Do you remember it? It always sat on the corner of her desk."

"Sorry. I wasn't in her office often enough to remember something like that. But a paperweight—it would be heavy. And blunt."

"It was rounded. Definitely rounded," I said excitedly. "And, Drew, it was missing! I remember thinking at first that the police had undoubtedly picked up everything in the room during their investigation and had probably just set it down in the wrong place. I'm sure I never found it. I know I would have noticed if I had."

I heard Drew sigh on the other end of the line. "So maybe it was the cat paperweight. So what?"

"Don't you see? The murderer must have taken it with him. All the police have to do is find the paperweight and they'll find the murderer. It will be easier as soon as we tell them what to look for."

"Get real, Ashlyn. They've got me. They're not interested in looking for anyone else anymore."

I am, I wanted to say. I wanted desperately to tell him about my suspicions. But I didn't dare. Not until I could prove something. Not until I went to Atlanta and checked things out for myself. And not until I could conduct my own search for the missing cat paperweight.

"Try to come over this weekend, will you, babe? I'm going out of my mind."

"I'll do my best," I promised, aching because I knew it was a lie.

I hung up and stared into the darkness. But what if I found the paperweight? And what if I discovered that all my suspicions about my mother were true? What would I do then?

chapter
19

The next day, after school, I came home to an empty house. My pulse began racing. Not because the house was empty. That was pretty common. But because I knew it was time for me to search for the cat paperweight. Surely if my mother had it, it would be in her room. After checking the garage and finding her BMW gone and putting my schoolbooks in my room, I stood at the bottom of the stairs and stared up at her bedroom door. It was closed. As usual. As if her room held a treasure trove of secrets.

"Mom!" I called out, just in case. No answer.

I tiptoed up the stairs and knocked. "Mom," I called again, having no idea what I'd say if she came to the door.

When there was no response I turned the knob and slowly opened the door. Stale cigarette smoke hung in the air and mingled with expensive perfume. The white satin drapes drawn at the windows and across the glass doors leading to the lanai balcony left the room in dusk. The only sound was the ticking of a gold-trimmed white porcelain clock that sat on her bedside table. I took a deep breath and cautiously stepped inside.

I glanced around at the room that looked so familiar and yet suddenly so strange. The bed, whose white satin spread made it look like a giant snowdrift, dominated the room. A gold-leaf armoire stood on the opposite wall, flanked by a pair of expensive antique chairs. As usual, nothing was out of place. Even the prescription bottles holding her sleeping pills and tranquilizers were lined up in a neat row beside the clock. *Where to start looking?* I wondered. The thought of disturbing the slightest thing made me cringe with dread. She would know someone had been in here. She never missed a thing. But I *had* to do it.

The armoire seemed the most logical place to begin. A delicate catch held the doors closed across the front. I carefully opened it and swung the doors open. What faced me was an array of drawers, small pigeonhole-size drawers across the top, larger drawers of varying heights below them.

I began slowly opening one drawer after another, feeling as much a thief as I had in Judy Rothlis's apartment a few days before. I found nothing among the silks and satins of her personal things, and I made certain that everything was just as I had found it before I closed one drawer and moved on to the next. I had no better luck in her closet or in the bathroom vanity.

I was standing in the center of her room, looking for another place to search, when I heard a car. I glanced out the window just as Mother's red BMW nosed into the garage.

I left her room and raced down the stairs to my own room, collapsing against the door in complete exhaustion as it closed behind me. My mind whirled with conflicting emotions. Maybe I had been wrong about her. Maybe her bringing me down to Florida from Chicago so near the time Mrs. Rothlis's baby was kidnapped was just a big coincidence, and I was about to make a big fool of myself trying to prove anything else. But another voice in my head reminded me that just because I hadn't found the cat paperweight in her room on the first try didn't mean that it wasn't there. Or wasn't in another hiding place.

The house seemed extra empty without Dumpster. I tried to tell myself that that was part of the reason I was having so much trouble getting out of bed every morning. He wasn't there to pat my face with a paw and purr softly in my ear. I supposed there were other reasons I was groggy, too. The fear over what I might find in Atlanta, coupled with the fear of what would happen to Drew if I didn't, kept me exhausted.

I almost missed hearing my alarm on Friday morning. In fact, I was more tired than I could remember ever being before. I finally dragged myself out of bed, but I felt as if I were moving in slow motion as I showered and got ready for school. I was still dropping weekend clothes and my makeup and blow-dryer into my overnight bag when I heard Keeley honking outside.

"I didn't even have time for breakfast," I complained as I threw my bag into the backseat and climbed into the convertible. "And all I had last night was a little bit of tuna salad I found in the fridge."

"I thought Greta fixed your dinner before she left for the day," said Keeley.

"She does, but she's taking a few days off," I said. "It's the pits. I hate cooking for myself."

"Here, have a doughnut," Keeley said, handing me a white paper bag with grease making transparent spots on the sides. "I got them to nibble on while we drive, but there's no reason you can't have one now."

I raised an eyebrow in her direction and pulled a chocolate-frosted doughnut from the bag. Toasting her with it, I said, "Here's to a great trip to Atlanta."

We attended all our morning classes, but at five minutes after noon we pulled onto Interstate 75, heading north. We knew we had until Monday morning to come up with a plausible excuse for why neither of us was in class that afternoon, so we weren't worried.

In addition to the doughnuts, Keeley had brought along a cooler of sodas, and we settled back to watch the monotonous countryside roll by while we listened to rock music stations, ate doughnuts, and drank sodas. In less than an hour we had passed Ft. Myers. In another hour we saw exit signs for Sarasota. By the time we saw the signs for Tampa, we had been on the road a little over three hours and terminal boredom was starting to set in. But we kept on going, stopping once for gas and to switch drivers and once at a drive-through hamburger place to get a bag of sandwiches and switch drivers again. It was almost eight o'clock at night when we finally rolled into a Holiday Inn at exit eight in Valdosta, Georgia.

"Oh," I groaned. "I've been sitting so long that I'm not sure I can stand up."

"Me, either," said Keeley. She did a couple of head rolls to relieve the tension in her neck and sighed. "Do we really have to go to Atlanta in the morning? Why can't we stop at one of the big factory-outlet malls along the interstate and shop instead?"

"Believe me, I'm tempted," I said.

But the next morning we were back in the car and on the road by seven A.M. When I hopped out of bed, my head felt surprisingly clear. I decided that it was probably the excitement of what lay ahead that gave me such a burst of energy. We stopped for an Egg McMuffin in Adel, Georgia, and passed the turnoff for Hartsfield International Airport on the southern edge of Atlanta at fifteen minutes before noon.

Instead of the sense of elation I had expected, the knowledge that I was finally there had a sobering effect on me. Part of me wished I had never found the death certificate or heard the story of the kidnapped baby, but another part of me knew I had to find out the truth.

We needed gas again, so while Keeley filled up, I went to the pay phone and looked up the address of *The Atlanta Journal-Constitution* in the phone book. It was the biggest newspaper in the Atlanta area, and its morgue should have what I was looking for—*if* it existed.

Marietta Street was easy to find, and an hour later I was sitting in a small booth with Keeley beside me, looking at microfilm of every paper printed in 1977. Since they were in chronological order, I pushed the button sending the months whirling by on the screen in a continuous blur, stopping every so often to be sure I hadn't gone past August. Stop. April, 17th. Stop. June, 9th. Stop. July, 23rd. Stop. July, 31st. Stop. August, 4th.

I held my breath. I was getting close. From that point on, I moved forward day by day.

"Is that it?" asked Keeley when I finally stopped on the edition printed August 17, 1977.

I nodded and looked at her. She was squinting.

"Where are your glasses?"

Keeley looked sheepish. "I left them in the car."

I turned back to the screen and began studying the tiny print. I was squinting myself, and it took a few minutes to discover that by turning a nob I could magnify the print.

Scanning down the front page, I mumbled, "The table of contents should be here somewhere."

I found it in rectangular box in the lower-left-hand corner. I ran a finger down the list. "There it is!" I said. "OBITUARIES, D10."

Scanning quickly through the pages again I found section D and a little farther on, page 10. I closed my eyes, feeling chills ghost-dance up my spine. This was it. The moment of truth. If someone named Ashlyn Marie Brennan had died here on August 17, 1977, I was about to read about it. *And then what?* I asked myself. *What if the person I think I am doesn't exist? Will I be able to handle that?*

Keeley tapped me gently on the shoulder and whispered, "Do you want me to look for you?"

I shook my head. "I'll be okay," I said. Then I looked at her and said earnestly, "It's harder than I thought it would be. You know, looking for my own death notice. You can't believe how funny it feels."

Keeley took one of my hands in hers and said, "I'm here for you, Ashlyn. You know that."

I nodded and let my glance slide from her face back to the screen. I had to look, and knew I might as well get it over with.

The entire page was filled with death notices, some in the form of obituaries and others listed as news stories. Slowly and carefully, I looked at every name.

My heart leapt. "It isn't here," I almost shouted to Keeley. "Look for yourself. There's nothing about a baby girl named Ashlyn Brennan. There aren't any baby girls at all. They're all old people, except for this one teenager killed on his motorcycle." I knew I sounded giddy, but I couldn't help it.

Keeley hadn't said anything. She was studying the page, too. Then she got this funny frown on her face that she always gets when she doesn't quite know how to say something.

"What is it?" I asked, dreading her answer.

"Well, I was just thinking that if the baby died on the seventeenth, it might have been too late to get into that day's paper."

I wanted to argue. To tell her that was ridiculous, but of course it wasn't. I should have thought of it myself.

"You're right," I mumbled so low that I wasn't sure if she heard me.

I slumped forward, rolling the pages down to the August 18th edition. This time OBITUARIES were on page D6. I caught my breath as I spotted an article

whose headline read: BABY GIRL DIES EN ROUTE TO FLOR-
IDA.

I swallowed hard and began to read, the words blur-
ring before my eyes.

> Efforts by local doctors failed to save the
> life of a five-month-old baby girl, Ashlyn
> Marie Brennan, who died of dehydration
> brought on by high fever. The baby's mother,
> Cynthia Brennan, 23, of Chicago, Illinois,
> who was traveling through the area on the way
> to join her husband in Florida, rushed the baby
> to the emergency room late yesterday, but the
> child died at 11:47 P.M. Doctors said the official
> cause of death was influenza.
>
> Mrs. Brennan told police that she had be-
> lieved her child's fever was caused by teething
> and only became alarmed when she could no
> longer bring it down herself.
>
> Burial arrangements are pending.

I sat there for a long time, staring at the screen, too
numb to move. I was vaguely aware of Keeley putting
her arms around me and gently rocking me. I heard
someone crying. I suppose it was me.

Later, when I was able to pull myself together, I
went back to the lady who had gotten the microfilm.
The nameplate on her desk said MRS. DORIS GOOCH, and

she was a thin woman, probably in her sixties, with her silver hair cut in a short Dutch bob. Mrs. Gooch looked up when I approached and smiled kindly.

"Did you find what you were looking for?" she asked.

I nodded. "Yes, and I was wondering if there is any way that I can get a copy of one of the articles."

"Sure is, but it will cost you a quarter," she said cheerily.

I dug a quarter out of my change purse and handed it to her, smiling gratefully. Then I led her back to the booth and pointed out the article I wanted.

It took less than five minutes to get the copy, but when I had thanked her and started to walk away it occurred to me that she might have some other information that I needed.

"Um, excuse me again, Mrs. Gooch," I said, turning back to her desk. "The baby who died in this article was a relative of mine. Is there any way I can find out where she's buried. I'd like to visit her grave."

"That information is on the death certificate over at the Department of Vital Statistics, but I'm afraid you'll have to wait until Monday to get it. All the government offices are closed on the weekends."

"Oh," I said, not bothering to hide my disappointment. "I'm just here for the weekend."

"That's too bad, but you can always write them and explain your situation. I'm sure they'd send a copy of the death certificate to a relative, and then you could visit the cemetery the next time you're in town."

I thanked her again and Keeley and I headed for her car.

"Can't you just see it now," I said as we got inside. "I'll write them, signing my own name, and tell them I'd like a copy of my own death certificate. Do you think it would shake them up?"

Keeley gave me a look that said she thought I'd gone over the edge this time and started the engine.

"Where to?" she asked.

"I don't know. Without the death certificate to tell us the cemetery where she's buried there isn't much else we can do here," I said.

"We could look up Mr. and Mrs. Jacobs. And Dumpster," she added quickly.

I gave her a sideways look. I knew what she was thinking. That if I really was the kidnapped baby, then they were my grandparents. I wasn't ready to face them under those conditions. "I didn't bring their address," I answered lamely.

"We might as well get a motel room," said Keeley. "It's four o'clock, pretty late to start back to Florida. Why don't we just relax tonight so that we'll be fresh in the morning."

"Good idea," I said halfheartedly.

We headed south on Interstate 75 again, deciding to get past the city before stopping. That way we could get a quick start in the morning without having to worry about traffic. At the Stockbridge exit we noticed a bunch of motel signs and found a room in an almost new Hampton Inn.

"What do you want to do?" asked Keeley after we'd checked in and brought our luggage into the room.

She was practically bouncing off the walls. I felt sorry for her, but I was beat. Finding my own death notice had been a real drag on my energy as well as my emotions. I didn't answer. Instead I pulled the article about the death of Ashlyn Marie Brennan out of my handbag and read it again.

"You know, Keeley, I keep thinking about that baby picture on Mrs. Rothlis's wall and wondering if it was me," I said. "It's such an eerie feeling. And if it was me, did she know it? Had she figured out where I was and come to get me? Or at least see me?"

Keeley stopped pacing the room and sank down in a chair. "Well, you said yourself that she seemed to pick you out at the beginning of the year to be her student aide. And you two did have an awfully special relationship."

"I know," I said. "She even encouraged me to talk about my home life. It must have been her way of finding out how I was getting along. Wow, Keeley, can you imagine how she felt? How much she must have loved me to have looked for me for so long?" I stared off into space. The heaviness in my heart was almost too much to bear.

"Ashlyn, I just thought of something." The urgent sound in Keeley's voice interrupted my thoughts. "What about your own baby pictures? Do they look anything like the picture Mrs. Rothlis had?"

I stared at her. "I don't . . . my mom . . ." I began, feeling as if a terrible secret was just being revealed to me. "There aren't any baby pictures of me, Keeley, not a single one in the house. My mom always said she hated sentimental stuff like that, and I guess I always believed her."

"Oh, sure," Keeley said contemptuously, "and she hates having her picture in the paper with the governor, too."

"I never really thought about it before," I said. "Especially since Dad always took pictures of me when he was home. He said taking them overseas with him made him feel that I was closer. Those are the only pictures of me that I can remember until I was old enough for school pictures. You don't think that . . ." The idea was too awful for me to say out loud. She hadn't wanted any pictures taken of me when I was a baby for fear they would somehow get into the wrong hands and link her to the kidnapping. Once I was older and having school pictures made, my looks had changed. It would be hard to prove that I was Heather Rothlis. That, plus the fact that the Brennan family was so prominent in the community, so far above reproach, gave her perfect cover for the terrible thing that she had done.

"I've got to see Dad's pictures," I said, scrambling off the bed to get the telephone credit card out of my purse. It would be the middle of the night in Egypt, but I didn't care. This was too important.

It took forever to place the call. I had to first go through the hotel switchboard, and then, because it was a hotel, she said I couldn't dial direct and she put me through to an international operator. I gave her the code for Egypt, which was twenty, and the code for Cairo, which was two, and then my dad's number at home, plus my credit card number, and waited. There were all sorts of gurgles and burps on the line as the call traveled halfway around the world to Egypt and my father finally answered.

"Hi, Dad. I'm sorry if I woke you."

"Ashlyn? What's wrong? Are you okay? Is your mother okay?"

"Everybody's fine," I assured him, looking at Keeley for support. "I'm really sorry I called so late, but I need to ask you a favor."

"Sure, sweetheart," he said. He sounded relieved. "I'm just glad nothing's wrong. What can I do for you?"

"I've got a project at school that I totally forgot about," I lied. "We're supposed to have a bunch of baby pictures, and you know how Mom's always been about pictures. She doesn't have a single one of me until I was in school."

"And you'd like me to send you some of mine?"

"Right. Ones taken before I was a year old. And if it isn't too much trouble, could you send them overnight to Keeley's house?"

There was silence at the other end. I crossed my fingers, hoping he wouldn't ask me why I didn't want them sent to me at home.

"I'll explain everything later," I said hopefully, "when you aren't paying for an international telephone call."

Dad laughed heartily. "Okay, sweetheart. I'll get them in the mail to you first thing in the morning. I miss you."

"I miss you, too," I said. "When are you coming home?"

"Not for a while, I'm afraid. We've got some trouble in the field."

"Okay," I said, "and, Dad. Thanks a *million*."

chapter
20

When Keeley pulled into the driveway at 10:15 P.M. Sunday, all the lights in the house were out except for the one in my parents' upstairs bedroom.

"Mom could at least have left the front door lights on for me," I grumbled. "She knew I'd be coming home tonight."

The instant I called her Mom, I caught my breath. It must have startled Keeley, too, because we sat staring at each other in the glow of the dash lights for what must have been only a moment but seemed much longer.

"Have you made a decision yet about what you're going to do?" she asked gently.

I shook my head. We had talked all the way home about the information we'd gotten at the newspaper, plus the clippings we'd seen in Judy Rothlis's scrap-

book, plus the death certificate. It proved, almost beyond a doubt, that I wasn't Ashlyn Brennan after all.

I had cried when I thought about Judy Rothlis. She
had been the kind of person I had always dreamed of
having for a mother. She had loved me so much that
she had spent sixteen years searching for me, and even
though I had been afraid to admit it while she was alive,
I had loved her, too.

But all the evidence we'd gathered didn't make my
mother—I mean, Cynthia Brennan—a murderer, even
though she had a terrible secret. There were still a lot of
things that didn't make sense. Why would she kidnap
me in the first place? And why would Judy Rothlis
confide in her about Drew's problem if she realized
who Cynthia Brennan was? Was it possible that Mrs.
Rothlis *didn't* know she had found her daughter? But
that couldn't be right, I argued with myself for the
hundredth time, because she left me the needlework
with Ashlyn Brennan's death certificate hidden inside.

I sighed wearily. "I just don't know. Maybe when I
see my dad's pictures I'll be able to decide."

Keeley gave me a skeptical look as I climbed out of
the car and said good night. I knew she thought I was
just putting off making a decision, but I couldn't help
it. My whole life was about to change, and I had to be
convinced that I was doing the right thing.

I couldn't take my eyes off the telephone as I settled
into my room again. I knew I should call Drew and at
least offer him an excuse for why he hadn't heard from

me all weekend, but I couldn't bring myself to do it. When I talked to him again, I wanted to be able to explain about everything. I wasn't ready to do that yet.

I didn't sleep at all that night. Cynthia was in the room directly overhead. I stared up at the ceiling. Was she awake? Had she heard me come home? But more than that, I couldn't stop wondering if she ever thought about what she had done. Was she sorry that she had stolen someone else's baby? Was that why I had never been able to get close to her? Did I remind her of the terrible crime she had committed? I rolled over, burying my face in my pillow. I wanted to cry again, but my tears had all dried up.

Keeley dropped me off at home after school the next day and then called a few minutes later to tell me that there was a package for me from my dad. I got to her house in record time, and she opened the door with a large padded envelope in her hand.

"Boy, when your dad said he'd send this right out, he meant it," she said appreciatively.

"Yeah, he's great."

I grabbed the envelope out of her hands and ripped it open. A cloudburst of photographs showered around my feet. For a moment I just stood there looking down at all those baby faces. Smiling faces. Crying faces. Faces looking at the camera in baby wonder. But gradually I knelt to sort them into two distinct groups.

"Look, Keeley," I said. "If you really study them closely, you can see a difference between these"—I gestured to a stack of pictures on my right—"and these"—I picked up the pictures on my left. "These were the ones when I was first born. They're the ones Mom—uh, Cynthia—sent to Dad. See on the back? She has the dates. They were all taken before I was five months old."

Keeley knelt beside me. She took them from my hand and nodded as she looked first at them and then at the other set. "The hair is brown, but in the early pictures it's darker."

"It's more than that," I said. "The shape of the face is different in the two groups. Don't you see it, Keeley? The older baby is the one Dad photographed himself, and her pictures look just like the baby picture Judy Rothlis had hanging on her apartment wall."

Keeley looked at me in wonder. "Ashlyn, do you know what this means. I mean, what it *really* means?"

I nodded. I couldn't stop the tears that welled in my eyes. "I'm Heather Rothlis," I whispered. "And do you know what else?"

"No," said Keeley. "What?"

"There's only one person besides Cynthia herself who might know why she stole me. Do you mind if I use your phone? I'll pay you back. I need to call Egypt."

This time I was able to dial straight through. I knew that over there it was the middle of the night again, but the phone rang so many times I was beginning to think I either had the wrong number or my father had gone away somewhere. Finally, he answered.

"Hi, Dad. It's me again. Sorry about the lousy timing."

He sighed patiently. "Sweetheart, I mailed the pictures just as you asked. I'm sorry if they aren't there yet. Hopefully you'll get them tomorrow."

"Oh, I got them already," I assured him. "Thanks a lot. They're just what I wanted. But now I need to ask you some questions. I'm really sorry it's the middle of the night over there. It's just that I've got this family history project for social studies due in a couple of days and I need some information about our family when I was a baby, and you know how Mom is. She doesn't really like to talk about such things."

Dad grunted in agreement. "I know how she is. I'll try to help. What do you need to know?"

I took a deep breath and plunged ahead. "Tell me about when Mom brought me home to Florida. Once she told me that she had been waiting in Chicago ever since before I was born for you to get home from Morocco. Then she got in the car and drove us down so that you could see me for the very first time? Is that really the way it happened?"

He didn't say anything for a moment. "Well, yes and no. But that's close enough."

Alarms were going off in my head. Just as I had

expected, there was more to the story, and I had to know what it was.

"Hey, that's not fair," I said, trying to sound as if I were teasing. "What do you mean, yes and no?"

"Well . . ." He hesitated. "I suppose you're old enough to know the truth. You realize by now that life doesn't always run smoothly."

"Right. So what happened?"

"Well, the truth of the matter is that I wasn't in Morocco when you were born. I was in Florida. You see, your mother and I were separated, and I had already seen my lawyer about filing for divorce. But as soon as you were born she began sending pictures of you to me." His tone softened. "I don't mind admitting that you were a beautiful baby, and the more pictures I received, the more I knew I had to see you."

He paused again, and I thought I heard him clear his throat. It was obviously hard for him to talk about it, but it was even harder for me to hear.

"Finally I called her and asked her to bring you down. I even told her that I might consider reconciliation for your sake. Even though I knew my work would keep me away from home a lot, I wanted to be with you whenever I could. It was a good arrangement for your mother, too. She had grown up in very modest circumstances, so in exchange for my being able to have my daughter, she would have the money and social position she craved so badly. I'm afraid it isn't a very pretty story, and I'm sorry for that. But I hope you'll never doubt how much I love you, Ashlyn."

Stunned, I replayed his words over again in my mind. Now I knew beyond a doubt why Cynthia Brennan couldn't tell him that their baby had died. Why she had stolen a baby she could never love. And why murder had been the only option when her secret was found out.

"I love you, too," I said as soon as I could regain my voice. "And, Dad? I need to ask you the most important favor that I've ever asked in my life."

"Of course, Ashlyn. I'll do anything for you that I can. What is it?"

I gripped the telephone receiver as salty tears rolled down my face. "Please, oh *please,* Dad. I need you. Will you come home?"

chapter
21

"You've got to call the police—*right now!*" insisted Keeley. Her voice was deadly serious, and she had taken hold of my shoulders and was looking straight into my eyes.

"I can't. Not until Dad gets here," I said. "He told me he'd make the fastest connections he could and be here in about forty-eight hours. I need for him to tell the police what he just told me. They'll be more likely to believe it if it comes from him. In the meantime, while I'm waiting for him to get here, I'll call Mrs. and Mrs. Jacobs in Atlanta and ask them to send Mrs.—I mean, my mother's scrapbook about the kidnapping. I'll also try to get a copy of Ashlyn Brennan's death certificate from the Bureau of Vital Statistics in Atlanta."

I paused, feeling suddenly sad. "Poor little Ashlyn,"

I said. "Just think, if she hadn't gotten sick and died on the way to Florida, none of this would ever have happened."

I wanted to say more but I didn't. I couldn't let myself think about what my life would have been like if I hadn't been kidnapped. If I had spent all these years as Judy Rothlis's daughter Heather. If I let myself think about that right now, I wouldn't be able to do the things I knew I had to do. There would be time later to deal with all that.

Over Keeley's protests, I went home.

"Aren't you afraid to be in the same house with her?" asked Keeley as I was leaving.

"Not really," I replied. "She doesn't have any idea that I know the truth. If I behave as normally as possible until Dad gets here, she won't get suspicious. Besides, she probably won't be home anyway."

I sounded braver than I really was. Opening that door and entering the house I'd lived in all my life was the hardest thing I'd ever done. It seemed to have suddenly changed, to be filled with secrets and mysteries I never knew existed. My pulse pounded in my ears. It was so quiet. So still. Even the regal white furniture seemed to be at attention, listening.

But I was listening, too. Listening for Cynthia. The sliding-glass doors were closed, locking out the comfortably familiar sounds of the waves lapping against the seawall in the canal and the palm fronds brushing against the screen of the lanai. Inside, there was nothing but silence.

I glanced up the stairs. The door to her bedroom was ajar, but no sounds came from inside. Breathing a sigh of relief, I tiptoed across the tile floor toward my room, stopping suddenly as I realized in a flash that this was the perfect time to make one more search of Cynthia's room for the cat paperweight.

A couple of minutes later, after making certain she wasn't home, I was standing in her room again. It looked exactly the same as it had before. Sterile white. Everything rigidly in place.

I glanced at the bed. I had never been in the room when Cynthia was lying in it, but I could imagine that she looked regal, even in sleep. A princess.

But I was in the princess's room to look for a paperweight. Round, like a pea. *The princess and the pea,* I thought and smiled at my own joke.

I went to the bed and lifted a corner of the white satin spread. People were always hiding things under a mattress.

"But a hard, round paperweight?" I argued. Still, I couldn't resist looking. "She might have stuck it in one of the corners, where she wouldn't roll over on it." I mumbled.

There was nothing under either of the corners at the foot of the bed, and I was just about to give up when I glanced up to the corner nearest her bedside table. I might as well look, I thought.

Pulling back the spread and the goose-down pillow in a satin case, I stuck my hand under the corner of the mattress and froze. My hand brushed against something. I knew instantly that it was not a paperweight, but something smooth and flat. Drawing it out, I stared in amazement at a file folder, and on the flap was the name: DREW JANSEN.

For an instant I couldn't breathe. So that was how she knew. Judy Rothlis hadn't told her about Drew. She hadn't shown Cynthia the file, either. Cynthia had stolen it. And she could have done that only if the counselor was powerless to stop her. Only if Judy Rothlis was dead.

Hugging the folder to my chest, I dashed out of the room and down the stairs to the kitchen. I couldn't wait any longer. I had to talk to Drew. But I had to do it in private instead of on the phone. And I had to make it look natural in case Cynthia found out.

Punching in the number for Shark River Marina, I cradled the phone on my shoulder and stretched out the cord as I went across the room and swung open the refrigerator door. While I listened to the ring, I searched for something to make a picnic supper.

I spotted a plastic container from the deli. The seal was broken, but when I opened it, it didn't look as if anything had been eaten out of it. I absently dipped a finger in, licking off chicken salad made with tarragon and toasted almonds. It was the deli's specialty and my absolute favorite.

"Shark River Marina, Drew speaking."

I cringed. I knew he would be angry.

"Hi, Drew. Can you talk?"

There was an instant of silence and then he exploded into the phone. "Ashlyn! Where have you been, for Christ's sake? You were supposed to come over this weekend?"

"I know, Drew, but—"

"You could have at least called," he stormed. "You knew how much I needed you."

"Drew, will you just listen? I'll pick you up in *Mellow Time* in forty-five minutes. Believe me, I'll explain everything then. I know who killed Mrs. Rothlis. Just be ready when I get there. Bye."

I hung up the phone and rummaged in the refrigerator again, pulling out another deli container, this one filled with pasta salad. I grabbed a bag of chips and a loaf of bread to add to the chicken salad and pasta salad and stuffed them in a grocery bag. A few paper plates and napkins and some cold drinks and I had our supper, which, I thought wryly, I'll probably be too nervous to eat. But we always took a picnic, and maybe doing something we always did would make it easier for me to deal with the seeming impossibility of what I had to tell him. Last, I stuffed the file folder into the bag with the food.

"Ashlyn? Is that you?"

I froze as Cynthia stepped into the kitchen from the living room. How long had she been standing there? Had she heard my conversation with Drew? Had she seen the file folder in my hand? I knew I had to act normal.

"Yeah, Mom," I mumbled, almost choking on the words. I was looking down, fumbling with the bag.

"Greta's still away so I picked up some cold salads from the deli for you to have—" She stopped. "What's in there?" she asked, pointing to the bag.

I tried to raise my eyes to meet hers. To look into the eyes of a murderer. Could I do it? I knew my face was flaming. I forced my eyes to flicker toward hers for an instant and then glance back at the bag.

"I found it . . . the food, I mean," I said. "Um, the weather's so great that Keeley and I decided to take *Mellow Time* out for a picnic. It's okay if I take the deli stuff along, isn't it?"

She nodded. "Have a nice time." Turning swiftly she left the kitchen and headed for the sliders leading to the lanai.

I slipped the folder out of the bag, leaving the food on the counter, and ran to my room to change into a swim suit, making sure the file and the photocopy of the article from the Atlanta paper were tucked safely into my beach bag before I grabbed the picnic supper and headed for the dock.

I squinted into the sky. It was generally clear, with only a few puffy clouds scurrying overhead, but an easterly wind was kicking up, whining in the rigging of my father's sailboat. *Oh, well,* I thought. *It doesn't matter. We aren't going far.*

It wasn't until I was aboard *Mellow Time,* heading toward the marina, that I allowed myself to sigh with relief over my encounter with Cynthia. It had gone pretty well, I decided. She hadn't suspected a thing, and I hadn't actually had to look her in the eye.

I also let myself imagine what Drew would think when I told him what I'd discovered. I knew he would be ecstatic that he was going to be cleared of the murder. But how would he take the news that I wasn't really Ashlyn Brennan? That instead I was the natural daughter of the woman who had died? And that Cynthia Brennan was the one who had committed the murder he was accused of?

Drew was waiting beside the gas dock when I pulled into the marina, his fists jammed into his jeans pockets and a scowl on his face.

I eased *Mellow Time* against the dock, and Drew jumped on board. Reversing the engines, I pulled away again and turned toward the open water.

"This had better be good," he said, shaking his head. "And what do you mean, you know who killed Mrs. Rothlis? If you turn on me, too . . ."

"I'm *not* turning on you," I insisted. "Keeley and I went to Atlanta last weekend. That's why I couldn't come over or even call."

"Atlanta!" His eyes were blazing.

"Just calm down and listen," I said. "No, better than that, there's something in my beach bag I want you to read."

I pulled out the copy of the obituary and handed it to him. I wanted to watch his face when he read it, but the Gulf waters were rough, and I had to keep tight control of the boat as it slapped against the waves.

By the time I had poured out the whole story, and showed him the file I had found under Cynthia's mattress, we had beached *Mellow Time* at Sand Dollar Island and were huddled together on the lee side of the island, eating our picnic supper, with a beach towel wrapped around our shoulders. Somehow telling the terrible secrets to Drew had given me a huge sense of relief, and I ate hungrily.

He hadn't said much. I could tell that he was turning it all over in his mind, trying to make sense of it, just as I had been doing ever since the terrible moment when I found my own death certificate. I watched him make himself a second sandwich, spreading the chicken salad on the bread as if he were in a trance and plopping another spoonful of pasta salad onto his paper plate. He ate slowly, staring into the surf where the wind had whipped the water into a froth and where a dozen or so sea gulls stood, solemn as a jury, facing into the wind.

Finally he turned and looked at me. His eyes were filled with sadness. "God, Ashlyn. I'm going to be okay, and I'm relieved and happy and all that stuff but

—I mean, how can you stand it, knowing *that she was your mother* and now she's dead?"

Instantly all of the pent-up sorrow came bursting out. I fell into his arms, sobbing. "Oh, Drew. I loved her so much. I really did, even though I thought she was just my counselor. I mean, she was so much like *me*. She never worried about how things looked or what people thought. She would have *hated* belonging to the country club. She was too mellow. But that's not all. We could talk. She listened and she cared."

"Of course she did," Drew said gently. He nuzzled my hair and rocked me. "You were her little girl, and she loved you enough to . . ."

Suddenly I felt his arms grow slack and he let go of me, falling backward and catching himself on one elbow.

"Whoa!" he said, pushing himself back up into a sitting position. "I don't know what happened. Hey, I don't feel so good." He reached out for me, but his hands were trembling, and his eyes didn't seem to be focused.

"Drew!" I screamed. "What is it! What's wrong!"

He couldn't seem to answer, and I scrambled to my feet, but a wave of numbness came over me, driving me to my knees. I fought against it, my arms and legs as heavy as lead.

"What's wrong?" I whispered frantically. "What's wrong with both of us?"

My eyelids felt as if they were being pulled downward by invisible strings. I shook my head, trying desperately to clear away the fog that was engulfing my mind.

Maybe if I just rest a minute, I thought, looking longingly at the cool, damp sand. *I'll just take a little nap, and then I'll feel better.*

I slumped against Drew. His skin felt cold and clammy. I was cold, too. We needed a blanket. Something to keep us warm while we rested. I reached for the beach towel, but it was too far away and too much troub . . .

"Ashlyn!" Drew's voice was just above a whisper, but the panic in it was unmistakable. "We gotta get outta here! We're gonna die! Cynthiathefoodwebeendrugged . . ."

chapter

22

At first my foggy mind refused to believe it. Drugged by my own mother? But Cynthia was not my mother, I reminded myself. And she had killed Judy Rothlis.

Suddenly I understood Greta's strange absence from the house the past few days. Cynthia must have given her time off so that she could gradually drug my food with her own tranquilizers and sleeping pills, and everyone would believe Drew had gotten me hooked on drugs. She must have overheard my call to Drew and seen the perfect opportunity to kill us both. With me dead, there would be no one to point a finger of suspicion at her regarding my mother's murder. With Drew dead, no one could dispute that he was a crazed drug addict capable of anything, including killing himself and the girl he loved.

But it was Cynthia who was capable of anything.

Still, it wouldn't matter if we didn't get back to shore, and I could feel the effects of the drugs growing stronger and stronger.

I forced my eyes to stay open and saw Drew struggling to get to his feet. The muscles in his jaw worked and the veins in his neck strained as he heaved upward. He swatted the empty air, grabbing for something to hold on to, but there was nothing there, and he sank to his knees with an exhausted grunt, his head lowered in defeat.

"Drew, let me help," I said. I crawled toward him, my own hands trembling now, but that simple exertion took my breath away. "I can't," I said. "I have to rest a few minutes."

Drew sat back on his haunches, breathing heavily as he looked at me. His eyes slipped in and out of focus. His mouth was open. His jaw slack.

"Ashlyn, you don't understand," he said, slurring his words. "We don't have a few minutes . . . there was enough stuff in there . . . we gotta get back . . . before we OD . . ."

Drew started for the boat on his hands and knees, but his arms gave way and he collapsed, his face pressed into the sand. He started again, and I crawled after him, reaching hand over hand and grabbing tufts of beach grass to pull myself along.

I didn't realize he had stopped again until I bumped into his feet. "Don't stop now!" I cried. "Keep going!"

His breathing was labored and he said in a raspy voice, "This isn't going to work."

"It will if we keep going," I insisted. "Go on!"

I shoved at him, but he didn't budge.

"Can you throw up?" he asked.

"I don't think so."

"You've got to. Stick your finger down your throat." He turned so that I could see his face, and jabbed a finger into his mouth to show me how. I closed my eyes, listening to him heave.

"Go on, Ashlyn! Make yourself gag. Get that stuff out of your stomach. Do it!"

I took a deep breath and plunged my finger down my throat, feeling first the awful tug at the back of my tongue and then the retching that seemed to turn my stomach inside out as a mass of sour food gushed into my mouth and spurted out onto the sand. Panting, I rolled onto my side and spit away the last particles of chicken and pasta, grimacing at the terrible burning taste left in my mouth and nose.

"Did it help?"

"No," I moaned.

I was telling the truth. I could barely keep my eyes open, much less hold my head up. Part of me didn't care. Through half-open eyes I saw a gull circling lazily overhead, and I let my head rest against the sand. It was so nice to lie here. If only I could go to sleep. Surely when I woke up everything would be okay again.

Wasn't everything always better in the morning? It would be dark soon. Already the rays of the setting sun were painting the horizon a ruby red. I could nestle down into the sand, burrowing until I had made a little nest to keep me out of the wind. It would be so nice just to curl up into a ball and let darkness surround me as I slept.

My eyelids fluttered and peace settled around me like protective arms. But as my eyes closed, a face appeared in my mind. A pale, angular face with cold eyes and gold hair glinting like a helmet. It was Cynthia Brennan, and she was smiling triumphantly at me.

I forced myself up. "Let's go! Let's get out of here!"

I wasn't sure if I had said the words out loud or only thought them, but I heaved myself forward across the sand in a last great effort to reach the boat. It looked so small and far away, like a miniature, bobbing in the surf.

Drew wasn't moving.

"Drew! Drew!" I screamed.

Panic gave me new strength. I crawled over by his head and grasped his hands between my knees. Digging my heels into the sand, I leaned backward and pulled. He moved. Scooting backward, I dug my heels in and pulled again. When I finally reached the water line, I leaned against the rocking bow of the boat to get my breath. The wind was strong out of the east, and the water swirling around me was startlingly cold. I shivered, and when a wave broke across Drew's still form, I saw him stir and his eyes slowly open.

"Oh, Drew, we can do it," I said through chattering teeth. "If you can just get up. The tide is out, so the water's shallow. If you can get to the swim platform, we can get you on board. Then you can help me up. I know we can do it if we work together."

By now the cold water had revived him a little more. He looked first at me and then at the boat. "I dunno," he said, shaking his head.

"We've got to try," I insisted. "Come on."

I stumbled to my feet and pulled him toward the stern of the boat where the water was only waist high. Without the paralyzing drugs in our system, getting aboard would have been a cinch.

I don't know how long we worked, holding on to each other, pushing, heaving, losing our grip on the wet, slippery swim platform and sliding backward into the water again, before Drew finally made it aboard. He put his arms over the gunwale and dragged himself up, falling onto the deck. I could hear him panting with exhaustion.

I reached upward for him to grab me and waited. Nothing happened. "Drew!" I screamed. "Don't lose it now! You've got to stay awake and help me. Drew, please! Where are you?"

He didn't answer. I tried not to let myself dwell on the fact that he had at least twice as much of the drugs in his system as I did. He had eaten two sandwiches to my one, and had taken a second helping of pasta salad. If I knew Cynthia, she had probably loaded both of the deli salads with enough drugs to kill a horse.

I called out to Drew again, but I knew he wouldn't answer. He had passed out again, and this time he might not wake up. It was up to me to get aboard, start the engines, and get us back to shore where we could get help.

Putting my arms on the platform and my foot on the boat's propeller, I squirmed and struggled. When I finally had the top half of me on the platform, I grabbed a metal cleat and got one leg up and then the other. I couldn't stop to look at Drew's still form lying on the deck. I had to get us out of there.

I had left the keys in the twin ignitions. I turned them and the two engines roared to life.

"Keep yourself steady. You can do it," I kept telling myself. "You've been boating all your life. You know what to do."

I put my hand on the throttle and glanced toward the bow of the boat, freezing. Stretching out from the tip of the bow, across the sand, and onto a knoll, was the anchor line.

"Oh, no," I whispered. Drew had buried the anchor there to keep the rough water of the Gulf from dislodging the boat and setting it adrift in the sea.

I quickly weighed my options. I couldn't go anywhere until the anchor was up. I didn't have the strength to climb out and pull it out of the sand, even though the electric winch would do the rest once it was loose, and Drew couldn't help. He was out cold.

"The radio!" The thought jolted me. How could I have been so stupid as not to have thought of it sooner? I flipped the switch turning it on and grabbed the mike. It was automatically set on Channel sixteen, the channel monitored by the U. S. Coast Guard for distress calls. Pushing the TALK button, I screamed. "Mayday! Mayday! This is *Mellow Time* beached on Sand Dollar Island. Mayday! Mayday! I need help—fast!"

I waited breathlessly for a response. Why didn't someone answer? I pulled the mike close to my mouth to transmit again when I felt something brush against my arm. I looked down in horror. It was the microphone cord, dangling from my hand. *It had been cut.*

"Oh, no! Oh, no!" I sobbed. I buried my face in my hands. I was running out of options fast.

No, I'm not! a voice screamed inside my head. *I'm going to get out of here if it's the last thing I ever do. I won't let Cynthia win! I won't let Drew die here! I won't! I won't!*

I grabbed the throttles again. I'd get rid of that anchor if I had to tear off the bow of the boat. I jammed the throttles into reverse as hard as I could. The engines roared, and *Mellow Time* surged backward and slammed to a stop as the slack came out of the anchor line and it held.

"Come on, come on," I pleaded under my breath, holding the throttles down hard. "Come on. You can do it."

I pushed the throttles into FORWARD and ran *Mellow Time* onto the beach again. Then I threw it into reverse, engines grinding as the boat bucked, trying to get away from the shore. I narrowed my eyes and watched the sand push upward in two long lines as the prong-shaped anchor gradually plowed its way toward the water and burst free.

Mellow Time slipped backward away from the beach, and I jammed the throttle forward and cut the engine speed.

"Okay," I told myself as I winched up the anchor and turned the boat toward home. "Just a little longer. That's all I have to hang on."

But as the adrenaline began to fade, the stupefying effects of the drugs took over again. My eyesight was blurry. My arms too heavy to hold on to the wheel. Maybe if I let loose, the boat would go on its own and beach itself somewhere along the wide stretch of public sand. Someone was always strolling on the beach, even at night. They would find us and go for help, and I could just sit back and rest and watch it happen.

My mind resisted. No, the seas were high and the current strong. We might be pushed back out to sea. Then they wouldn't find us until it was too late. Cynthia would win.

Exhaustion swept over me in waves, paralyzing my body and my mind. It was dark now. I looked around in despair. We were heading for shore, but the lights of the condos along the beach looked miles away. The buildings glowed like giant birthday candles.

My mind cleared for an instant. The flare guns were in the emergency gear compartment near my feet. If I could get one, load it, and set it off, someone onshore might see it and go for help. I scrambled to open the compartment and pull out the gun. I tried to jam a cartridge into the chamber, but my hands felt dead and the size of boxing gloves. I tried again. This time the cartridge went in, and I snapped the barrel shut. It took all my strength to raise the gun above my head and cock it. I fumbled until my finger found the trigger.

With one last burst of energy I squeezed and heard the deafening shot. The flare rose into the air like a rocket, and a burst of red lit up the sky and hung like a giant umbrella over my head.

Sighing, I lowered the flare gun into my lap. The birthday candles were coming closer, but I couldn't watch them anymore. My eyes were closing. I was drifting away, off on a misty wave.

It was quiet for a while, and then someone was shouting. I couldn't make out much of what he was saying.

The last words I heard were "This is the Coast Guard . . ."

chapter
23

When I woke up in the hospital, my father was standing beside my bed.

"You're going to be all right, sweetheart," he said, bending to kiss my cheek. Tears glistened in his eyes.

"Oh, Daddy, I'm so glad to see you," I whispered. Then I added, "What about Drew?"

"He's fine, too," said Dad. He explained how the Coast Guard had taken us to shore and rushed us to the hospital.

I nodded contentedly when he finished the story. I was still groggy, and my head ached. I just wanted to go back to sleep, but a sudden rush of memories made me sit up with a start.

"What about—"

Dad gently shushed me. "It's all right," he said soothingly. Frown lines creased his face. "Keeley told me everything. Your moth—Cynthia is in jail and she's confessed to the murder of Judy Rothlis and to the attempted murder of you and Drew. I'm so sorry, Ashlyn. I should never have let my business keep me away from home so much. If I had been around more I might have seen . . ." He shook his head sadly.

"It's not your fault," I insisted. "Besides, nobody could possibly have suspected she'd do the things she did. I mean, it's just too bizarre."

"I guess we can't change what happened now, can we?" Dad glanced toward the door. "Are you up to company? There's someone out in the waiting room I'd like you to meet. He has something important to tell you."

"Sure," I said. "But what is it about?"

"I'll get him, and let him tell you himself."

The moment the tall, thin man walked into my room, I knew who he was. He was middle-aged, thin, with short dark hair, a perfect match to the description of the man Judy Rothlis's next-door neighbors had seen visiting her apartment the evening before she was killed. He was the mystery man I'd wanted so desperately to find.

I must have looked alarmed, because Dad rushed to me and said, "It's okay. He's a private detective. Mrs. Rothlis hired him. Listen to what he has to say."

The man nodded courteously to me. "Hello, Miss Brennan. My name is Greg Fitz and I'm a private detective, like your dad said. First, let me say how sorry I am about all of this. I just wish I'd realized that she was in danger. Maybe I could have done something."

My heart was in my throat. "I'm sure you would have, Mr. Fitz. What was it you wanted to tell me?"

Greg Fitz pulled a chair close to the bed and sat down. He took a deep breath, as if what he was about to say was painful.

"I had worked for Judy Rothlis on and off for several years while she lived in Tampa and taught in the school system there. Every time she saw someone who looked like Sally Grant, or she thought she had any kind of clue, she would call me, and I'd do my best to check it out. I guess it was about a year and a half ago when she saw Mrs. Brennan's picture in the Tampa paper along with an article saying she was giving some kind of talk on environmental issues. Judy called me, all excited. She said that Mrs. Brennan looked so much like Sally Grant that she had gone to the talk and was almost convinced that she was the woman who had stolen her baby. She wanted me to see what I could find out about Mrs. Brennan."

Mr. Fitz shifted in his chair, leaning forward as he went on with his story. "Of course, what I found out was that Mrs. Brennan was a prominent woman, above reproach, and rich as all get-out."

Mr. Fitz grinned nervously at Dad. "Sorry, sir. That just slipped out."

"That's all right, Mr. Fitz," said Dad, smiling in amusement. "Please go on with your story."

"Well, it didn't seem likely to me that a woman like Mrs. Brennan would steal anybody's baby. Of course I did find out that she had a daughter"—he nodded toward me—"who was the same age as Judy's little girl would be, and that was all she needed to hear. The next thing I knew, she had a job down here and was moving."

"But if she knew back then that I was her daughter, why didn't she do something about it?" I asked.

"She didn't know for sure," said Greg Fitz. "She needed proof. Besides, as badly as she wanted you back, she didn't want to disrupt your life if you were happy."

"So that's why she always seemed so interested in my problems," I said.

Mr. Fitz nodded slowly. "That's right. And when you told her that you had been born in Chicago because your father was overseas, and your mother brought you to Florida when you were five months old, she felt sure she was on the right track. She called me in Tampa and asked me to search the records around Atlanta to see if I could find out what happened to the real Ashlyn Brennan. A couple of days later I drove down here and handed her a copy of Ashlyn Brennan's death certificate. She told me that night that she was going to ask Cynthia Brennan to come to her office on the pretext of discussing a problem you were having at school. She wanted to meet Mrs. Brennan face to face and size her up before she made up her mind what to do. She wanted to see what kind of woman had raised her daughter."

"And Cynthia must have recognized her and panicked," I murmured. "But why didn't she figure out who Judy Rothlis was sooner? Shouldn't she have recognized the name? Rothlis isn't all that common."

My dad walked over and put an arm around my shoulder. "I think she had put the entire kidnapping out of her mind a long time ago. At the time it happened, she did what she thought she had to do, and that was the end of it. Remember, having money and being socially prominent were the most important things in the world to her. I'm sure that after all this time she thought nothing could touch her."

I nodded and sank back against the pillow. Judy Rothlis had put the needlepoint poem into her will when she felt sure I was her daughter. She had probably put the death certificate inside the backing for safekeeping and in case something went wrong during her appointment with Cynthia Brennan. I was going to have a lot to deal with emotionally, I thought, and it was going take a long time.

It has now been six weeks since that terrible night when Drew and I were rescued by the U.S. Coast

Guard. All charges have been dropped against Drew, and Cynthia is in jail awaiting sentencing for the murder of Judy Rothlis. She won't stand trial because once all the evidence against her had been produced, she confessed. She admitted that when Judy Rothlis threatened to go to the police and accuse her of kidnapping her baby sixteen years ago, she picked up the cat paperweight on the counselor's desk and hit her with it. The murder weapon was never found because she took it to Tallahassee when she went to see the governor and disposed of it there.

The worst moment came when I visited her in jail and she turned on me, saying that she could never love me because I was a poor substitute for the baby she had lost. But in a way, it was the best moment, too. It finally explained why I could never please her, and it liberated me from her once and for all. It set me free to be Heather Rothlis in my heart and to realize that even though Judy Rothlis is dead, I really did have the one thing I had always longed for—a mother who loved me.

Dad and I are making a new start, too. I reminded him that a real dad is the one who loves and takes care of you, so it doesn't matter that I'm not his natural child. He liked that and plans to spend less time abroad and more time with me.

He likes Dumpster, too. Mr. and Mrs. Jacobs—or I should say, my grandparents—said they just couldn't adjust to a pet in the house and gave him back to me. That's what they said, but I think they love him just as much as I do and simply wanted me to have him.

Even the house seems different. Once in a while I enter a room and expect to see Cynthia there, stubbing out one cigarette and lighting another. Then I remember that she's gone and she'll never be back. But most of the time the whole place just feels cheerier and brighter. Dumpster has the run of the house, and Greta is slipping him so many goodies that he's getting fat. Keeley comes over a lot now, too. That's something she never felt comfortable doing before.

That brings me to Drew. He's gone into another rehab program. I still love him and hope and pray that this one will work, but I'm realistic, too. We have a lot to overcome before we can think about a future together. As the old saying goes, only time will tell.

I hung my mother's needlepoint poem above my bed so that Dumpster and I can look at it each night before we go to sleep. I've memorized the words by now because they are so special.

GOD GIVES EACH ONE OF US

ONE DEAR MOTHER

SO THAT NOBODY NEED FEEL SLIGHTED

AND ONLY ONE

SO THAT NOBODY NEED FEEL TOO PROUD.

about the author

Betsy Haynes is the author of more than fifty novels for young people, including the Taffy Sinclair books, The Fabulous Five series, *The Great Mom Swap, The Great Dad Disaster,* and *The Great Boyfriend Trap.* Her other books include award winners *Cowslip* and *Spies on the Devil's Belt.* When she isn't writing, Betsy loves to read mysteries and to travel. She and her husband, Jim, also spend as much time as possible aboard their boat, *Nut & Honey.*

The Hayneses live on Marco Island, Florida, and have two grown children, two keeshond dogs, and a black cat with extra toes, who was the inspiration for Dumpster.